The Lotus Caves

The Lotus Caves

JOHN CHRISTOPHER

Aladdin

NEW YORK LONDON TORONTO SYDNEY NEW DELHI

This book is a work of fiction. Any references to historical events, real people, or real places are used fictitiously. Other names, characters, places, and events are products of the author's imagination, and any resemblance to actual events or places or persons, living or dead, is entirely coincidental.

ALADDIN

An imprint of Simon & Schuster Children's Publishing Division
1230 Avenue of the Americas, New York, NY 10020
This Aladdin paperback edition November 2014
Text copyright © 1969 by John Christopher
Cover illustration copyright © 2014 by Anton Petrov
Also available in an Aladdin hardcover edition.
All rights reserved, including the right of reproduction in whole or in part in any form.
ALADDIN is a trademark of Simon & Schuster, Inc., and related logo is a registered trademark of Simon & Schuster, Inc.
For information about special discounts for bulk purchases, please contact Simon & Schuster Special Sales at 1-866-506-1949 or business@simonandschuster.com.
The Simon & Schuster Speakers Bureau can bring authors to your live event. For more information or to book an event contact the Simon & Schuster Speakers Bureau at 1-866-248-3049 or visit our website at www.simonspeakers.com.
Cover designed by Karin Paprocki
Interior designed by Hilary Zarycky
The text of this book was set in Venetian 301
Manufactured in the United States of America 1014 OFF
2 4 6 8 10 9 7 5 3 1
Library of Congress Control Number 2014946003
ISBN 978-1-4814-1838-6 (hc)
ISBN 978-1-4814-1837-9 (pbk)
ISBN 978-1-4814-1839-3 (eBook)

To Julia
for the spark that broke the log-jam

Contents

I

The Bubble

MARTY HAD TO GO ALL THE WAY ACROSS the Bubble every morning, since school and his parents' apartment were both on the perimeter but almost exactly opposite. This did not present much of a problem: he only had to walk a hundred yards to pick up an autocabin. After that he punched his destination on the dial and the robots took over, swinging the cabin out onto the overhead moving cable and plotting the course which would take him most directly to the school depot. He had timed it once at twenty and a half minutes, and knew it would never vary by more than seconds. It could have been a bore but he usually had enough homework held over to pass the time. The dial panel served as a desk; fairly stable except when the cabin swung out onto a new line with a jerk that sent his stylo skittering across the plastic. That sometimes meant blanking out several lines and rewriting them.

Morning was Earth-time, of course. The sun took fourteen days to arc its way across the sky above the Bubble, its glare reduced but not eliminated by the film sprayed on the inside of the huge transparent dome, and then for another fourteen days there was night, the stars and the bright globe of Earth surrounded by the deep blackness of space. That was how it was now but the long lunar night was approaching its end. Tomorrow the sun would be up.

A minute before the journey's end the dial pinged softly at him. Marty set about gathering his things. He looked out of the side and saw a boy from his class, Ben Trillici, in a cabin that was on a line converging with his toward the school run-in. There was some fun in gauging which would hit the relay first and slide through while the robot controls held the second cabin back. His was the one that made it, and he gave a thumbs-up sign and grinned. Other cabins were coming in and he checked them over to see if Paul was in one. He was not, though. Marty's guess was that he was already in school; he himself was a couple of minutes later than usual.

It was only at assembly that he realized Paul must be away. He was surprised at that. They had visiphoned the previous evening about a problem in math, and he had seemed O.K. then. Moon-sickness, of course, could come on you pretty quickly. (Even after nearly fifty years of people living in the Bubble the doctors did not understand it completely: they said it was partly a disturbance of the inner ear, partly psychological.) It would have to be Moon-sickness. Owing to the barrier precautions and the isolation there were no other forms of illness. In films he had seen people on Earth suffering from things like flu and head colds, and wondered what it must be like to have to cough and sneeze like that.

The first class was history. They were doing the Roman Empire and Mr. Milligan, the teacher, ran a reconstruct film on the screen. You saw a Roman family on the day of a triumph, watched the yawning slaves prepare breakfast as the deep blue sky paled behind the roofs of the villa, heard the creak of oxcart wheels in the narrow streets where the stone, through the long years, had worn into deep ruts. The family itself consisted of father and mother and five children, two boys and three girls. One of the boys was about Marty's age. He ate figs and crusty bread for breakfast, washing it down with watered wine, and was dressed in a toga which he had just become old enough to wear. Dawn had broken over the city of Rome, and the sun was a soft gleaming gold in powder blue.

Marty let his gaze stray from that scene to the windows of the classroom. Mr. Milligan had not blanked them; teachers rarely did during the lunar night. They looked through the transparent wall of the Bubble to the plain and distant mountains. Nothing moved or changed there. In the brightness of Earthlight one saw the stretch of flat blackness and the faraway jagged peaks. One or two of the high points dazzled white; signs of a different kind of dawn.

He came back to the film. With the sound track muted, Mr. Milligan was pointing out things of which they ought to take special note: the atrium with its tinkling fountain, the triclinium with couches along three sides of the great dining table. Then the family set out, attended by slaves, for the Senate stand from which they would watch the procession. The girls and their mother rode in litters but the senator and his sons walked through the colorful and now crowded streets. In schools on Earth, Marty gathered, reconstruct films gave you the smell of the scene in addition to sight and sound. He had asked his father why this was not done on the Moon—was it a technical problem? Not technical, his father had said, but a matter of policy. Smell was the most powerful of all the senses, and they did not think it advisable.

English followed. They were on the late nineteenth-century Romantic poets. Mrs. Kahn read Swinburne to them:

The full streams feed on flower of rushes,
Ripe grasses trammel a travelling foot,
The faint fresh flame of the young year flushes
From leaf to flower, and flower to fruit;
And fruit and leaf are as gold and fire,
And the oat is heard above the lyre,
And the hoofed heel of a satyr crushes
The chestnut-husk at the chestnut-root . . .

Streams, he thought—rushes, grasses standing high by a riverside and full of flowers, trees breaking into leaf in spring after a long winter . . . He knew what they were. He had seen them on television and the movie screen. He had even seen one fantasy film in which satyrs ran wild through a sunlit glade.

He felt a bit lost at recess. Paul and he usually gossiped about TV, or continued one of their interminable games of chess, or just sat about idly and companionably. They kept more or less to themselves. Although everybody knew everybody in the Bubble, people made one or two friends and stuck to them. This morning Marty was on his own. So was Steve du Cros, but he nearly always was alone. He was an orphan, both his parents having been killed in a launch explosion when he was five or six, and a loner. He was not much liked and gave the impression of not minding that: he had a sharp tongue. The teachers were not enthusiastic about him either. He often broke rules and always gave the impression that he might be just going to.

Then, with recess almost over, Marty saw Paul come in at the door. All Lunarians (the name given those who had been born on the Moon) were taller than they would have been on Earth, but Paul was more so than most—a six-footer at fourteen. He had a thin gangling frame and a face that was ugly except when he smiled. That was his usual expression though, and he smiled now, catching sight of Marty. But there was something else in his look, something odd.

Marty said: "How is it? I thought you must have the sickness."

Paul shook his head. "I'm fine."

"Then how come you missed the first two classes? Not that there was anything to miss."

"I had to see old Sherrin. Dad brought me in."

Sherrin was the principal. Marty asked curiously: "What about? Flunking physics in the last exams?"

"No."

There was something which he seemed both eager and reluctant to tell. Marty said impatiently: "Then what?"

"My folks have decided that . . . They're sending me down."

Sending down meant only one thing, one destination: the globe lighting the black sky above their heads. Marty could not believe it. He said: "But why?"

Paul shrugged. "Some medical stuff."

"And when?"

"Next flight."

"That's . . ."

"Yes," Paul said. "Next week."

Marty thought about it in the cabin going back, about the whole business of living in the Bubble and what it meant. Those who came here did not go on home leave: the cost of transporting a human being across a quarter of a million miles, although less than it had once been, was still fantastic. You contracted, usually in your early twenties, for twenty-five years' service. At the end of that time you retired to Earth, with enough money to make your retirement years easy, even luxurious.

This meant living for a quarter of a century under the unnatural artificial conditions which the Moon enforced. As much as possible was done to make them tolerable. There was family life, for instance. Men and women were recruited in roughly equal numbers, with a preference for married couples or those engaged to be married. They could have children, though large families were discouraged. The children grew up in the Bubble, never knowing anything else except at second hand on a screen. At any time after early childhood parents could, if they chose, decide to send them down—send them back to Earth. The snag was that the trip was one-way and once only. Parents and child would not see each other again, except on the expensive inter-world visiphone link, until the end of the parents' tour of duty. For Lunarians sending down also involved several weeks of conditioning on Earth in a special unit, with gravity slowly built up to full Earth strength and muscles trained to bear the extra weight.

Marty, like Paul, was fourteen. He had been born in the Bubble five years after his mother and father had come to the Moon. Their contract had six more years to run. There had been some talk of his going back to an Earth university when he was nineteen, which would be a year before their return. He had never thought of going down earlier. But neither, so far as he knew, had Paul.

His mother was in the apartment when he arrived. She had a job outside the family, as everyone in the Bubble did, but her duties in the Food Programming Section were geared to fit in with Marty's school day. She looked tired—more so than usual. She smiled and kissed him, and asked him how school had been. He wondered if she would say something about Paul—news traveled almost instantaneously around the Bubble—but she did not. Because of that, he said nothing either. They talked about ancient Rome; she said it had been her favorite period of history when she was a girl.

He asked her: "Did you ever get to visit there? Rome, I mean?"

She nodded. "We spent a year there once. Father—your grandfather—had lived there when he was an art student."

"What's it like?"

"Oh, well . . ." She looked at him. "You've seen modern Rome in the films. That one last week."

"I know. But I mean—what's it really like?"

She looked away from him. "It's so long ago, Marty. I don't remember properly." She looked through the window toward the ramp. "I think that's your father."

Marty glanced at his finger-watch. "It's too early for him."

"He said he might get away early today." The door opened, and she said with what sounded like relief: "Hello, darling."

They kissed, and his father said: "Hi, boy. They let me off the leash half an hour before time. How about you and me heading up to the reservoir and catching us two or three trout for supper?"

• • •

The reservoir, like the park in which it stood, was one of the things intended to make life more natural. Keeping the recirculated water of the Bubble in this small open lake meant an extra cost in filtering and purifying plant. All such costs had to be very carefully considered. The Moon colony did what it could toward paying its way by mining and refining precious metals which were rocketed back to the mother planet, but apart from that its value lay in the less commercial fields of astronomical, selenographic and interplanetary research. The taxpayers back home footed the bill, and there was small scope for luxuries. This one, though, was regarded as justifiable. The water in the lake was only a degree or so below the Bubble atmospheric temperature of 18° centigrade, and trout flourished in it. Anyone who wanted to fish for natural protein was at liberty to do so. Other fish were grown in tanks. Meat came from the factory farm, with battery chicken as the mainstay.

Marty and his father made their way through the park to their usual fishing spot. There were four carefully trimmed lawns, flower beds and borders, a clump of shrubbery. Everything was cal-culated for economy and for the carefully planned balance of life in the Bubble. The flowers were specially bred to last and all the shrubs were ever-greens: deciduous plants could have been trained to adapt to a world with no seasons, but their falling leaves would have been a nuisance.

The lake had been constructed asymmetrically, in a distorted kidney shape. The Bubble itself had to be a regular hemisphere, but as far as possible things inside it were given irregular shapes and lines in an attempt to avoid monotony. Even so, even with a part of its rim left in the irregular black basalt of the Moon's natural surface, the pool could not seem anything but artificial. Anyway, there was not an inch of its border, of any place inside the Bubble, that was not as familiar to Marty as the walls of his bedroom. Nothing changed. Changing things would have cost money.

They fished in silence for a time. During lunar night the Bubble was artificially lit by high-poled lamps which were faded out toward the end of the twelve-hour day through a rheostat at the electricity plant. At the moment they were still fully lit. Marty could see the others fishing around them, twenty or thirty, each in the place to which he came automatically. He thought of a feature film he had seen on TV about salmon fishing in Norway, with a thigh-booted man standing out in a torrent that foamed around his legs, and the valley empty to the distant gray horizon.

His father said: "You heard about Paul."

It was not a question. Marty nodded. "Yes, he told me."

"I was talking to his father today. There's a medical factor involved. You know what a long streak Paul has turned into. They've always known that rehabilitation to Earth gravity is tougher on tall Lunarians—it's pretty obvious why—and recently they've come to the view that if you leave things too late you get permanent posture trouble. The doctors think Paul's that sort of case."

"I see."

"The Millers aren't happy about it, but they have to put his health first, of course. They've only got three years of contract to run, but it's a long time."

Marty asked: "Where will he be living, on Earth?"

"With his grandparents in California. Just outside San Francisco."

"Sounds like a good place. We've been doing the United States in geography."

"Pretty good. I'm from New England myself."

Marty knew that, and also knew it was something his parents did not normally talk about. In the Bubble there was a good deal of general talk about Earth—about what TV showed was happening there—but people did not speak much about their own earlier lives.

After a pause, his father said again: "The Millers have only three years to go themselves. That helps."

"I suppose it does."

His father cast, and the line floated out across the placid, unrippled waters. He said: "Fifty generations of fish that have never seen a real fly but they still rise to the lure. This is a tricky problem, Marty. I've not talked about it before because it's just about impossible to explain it. Some people send their children down when they're four or five. That means they grow up as strangers, with strangers.

There's a case for it. You can make a case for doing it at any age. The Dickinsons sent Clive when he was twelve because that was the age for entry to Peter Dickinson's old boarding school in England.

"We gave it a lot of thought, your mother and I. We decided to keep you till you were ready for a university. Maybe we were being selfish—I don't know. One of the arguments on our side was that you and Paul were such buddies—had been since you crawled around a sandpit together, before you could walk. I guess that one has kind of blown up in our faces."

Marty did not say anything. His father went on: "We've been thinking about things again. We decided you are old enough to make a decision for yourself. If you want to go down, we'll fix it."

"Where would I live?"

"We've got relatives in different places. You could have a choice."

His father had spoken evenly and casually, but Marty realized there was nothing casual about this, nor about the decision he should make. He was excited, and guessed the excitement could have shown in his voice. He was a bit ashamed and, realizing that, realized something else—that it really would mean leaving them, for six long years. He would be down on Earth and they would be still up here in the Bubble. He imagined seeing his mother's anxious face, not in reality but on the flickering circle of the visiphone screen, rationed to a few minutes at a time. He said quickly: "It doesn't matter. I don't want to go down."

"You're sure of that? You could give it thought. You don't have to make your mind up right away."

"I'm sure," he said. "I'm fine here."

"Then I'm very glad. Especially on account of your mother. Life here is more of a strain on some people than others. They miss things more, things they knew back on Earth. Your mother does."

But you don't, Marty thought with sudden resentment. He looked at his father's tall, upright figure, the strong chin, high-cheekboned face, steady gray eyes. You're happy enough here.

"It would have been rough for her if you had decided to go. It's going to be pretty rough for Mrs. Miller."

The excitement had gone; in its place there was a sick feeling in his stomach. He had been offered the trip to Earth and had turned it down. He was stuck with the Bubble.

His father said: "Hey, you're not watching your line! That looks like a big one."

He went with the Millers by crawler to the launch station. It was six miles away along the edge of the Sea of Rains, as a precaution against blowups damaging or maybe even destroying the Bubble. The caterpillar tracks took them steadily with occasional jolts across the Moon's surface, from time to time plunging through dust pockets and sending dust scattering on either side, a shower of floating sparks in the rays of the risen sun.

Nobody spoke much. At the launch station they went on board with Paul and saw him for the last time, with all of them crowded together in the capsule. There was the bunk in which he would lie, cushioned for takeoff. And for landing. It was hard to believe that in a few weeks he would be breathing the air of Earth, not inside a protective dome but out of the whole wide sky of the planet.

Paul said: "You'll write to me. I'm counting on that."

"Sure," Marty said. "You, too. If you don't find you have too many other things to do."

But he would, of course. Paul said: "I won't. Bye, Mom, Dad. I'll visiphone you right away, soon as I land."

Mrs. Miller kissed Paul. Mr. Miller put a hand on his shoulder, squeezing hard. Then they had to get out and take a cabin across to the control center. From the viewing level they heard the relay of the countdown, and saw the exhaust gases rise in a fiery cloud from the pit before the ship itself began to rise, sliding out of its sheath, slowly at first and then faster and faster until it was a gleaming, vanishing speck in the sky. That was when Mrs. Miller started crying.

She had stopped by the time they took the crawler back to the Bubble, but the silence was worse than on the way out. Marty left them at the main airlock to make his way home. Mr. Miller said: "Thanks for coming along, Marty."

Mrs. Miller said: "You'll come and see us still?" Her hands held his lightly. "We wouldn't like to lose touch with you, Marty."

As if one could lose touch with anyone inside the confines of the Bubble. He said: "I won't lose touch, Mrs. Miller."

2

The Great Balloon Crime

MARTY FOUND IT EVEN WORSE THAN HE had expected. He went around to the Millers for Paul's first visiphone call, and was already restless from three days of mooching about, wondering what to do and whom to talk to. The screen's circle showed Paul's head and shoulders and, fuzzily, the room behind. He realized he had had some fantastic notion that there would be a landscape—trees and stuff—but of course Paul was in the rehabilitation center, under artificial gravity. The room was very little different from rooms here.

Conversation was strained and awkward. Halfway through contact was lost in a burst of static which drowned sound and vision for half a minute or more. Mr. Miller was swearing under his breath: you got no extra time for loss of picture. When it had cleared up, Paul said to him: "I set up my chess set for that game we were playing. I'll mail you my next move."

Mail came in with the supply rockets, photographically reduced onto transparencies which you read through a magnifier. The schedule was roughly three in two months. It was going to take a long time to finish the game.

Marty said: "Fine. You're going to lose that castle, whatever you do."

The seconds ticked on. In a way the five minutes of the call dragged, and in a way it seemed to be over almost as soon as it began. The circle flashed and died in the middle of a sentence from Paul. Mr. Miller said heavily: "That's that," and switched off. It would be a month before their next contact. It was not just a question of cost: the channels were needed for scientific and administrative communications and private calls were strictly rationed.

By the next call, or at least by the one after that, Marty thought, Paul would be out of the rehabilitation center, living a normal life. An Earth life. He said: "Thanks for letting me sit in, Mr. Miller. Hope I didn't hog things too much."

Mrs. Miller said: "Can't you stay awhile, Marty?"

"Afraid not. I've got a whole load of homework needs doing."

That was true, but he did not head back home right away. He felt restless and frustrated. He thought a workout in the gym might help, and dialed a cabin to the Recreation Center. It was near the middle of the Bubble, one of the tallest buildings, with six floors between the gym in the lower basement and the Starlight Room on the roof, which was the one place people could go out to dine. You cooked your own food on the infra and prepared your own wine from instant, but at least the setting was different. A little different, anyway.

He found he had hit a bad time. The exercising machines were all full with people waiting, and the pool was crowded also. There was a little more room on the bars, but he found he had soured on the idea of exercise. It seemed better to go upstairs and take in part of the current movie at the ground-floor theater. He had seen it already, and not thought much of it, but he had an idea he would feel less surrounded. He went up the stairs in float jumps, touching down on every fourth or fifth step.

He stuck the film for five minutes before boredom drove him out. He ought, he knew, to take a cabin home and start demolishing that homework. Instead he went up two more floors to the library and study rooms. At least it would be quiet and there might be a chance of being alone. There were three or four people in the library itself and he went through to the rooms beyond. Of the six available, all but one showed the red light outside signifying "Occupied—Don't Disturb." He pushed open the door of the sixth and realized there was someone there too. Steve du Cros sat at the table and was busy writing. He looked up, annoyed.

Marty said: "Sorry. I guess . . . You didn't put the light on."

"Didn't I?" Steve was stocky for a Lunarian, a

little shorter than Marty and more powerfully built. His face was broad but sharp-eyed. He had black curly hair and blue eyes, slightly protuberant behind contacts.

"You want to use the place?" He closed his pad. "That's O.K. I'm about finished."

"No, it's all right. I wasn't doing anything really. Were you writing that book review for English? It's not due till Monday, is it?"

"No, it's something of my own." He paused. "I'm writing a book."

Marty was surprised, but the surprise diminished with reflection. Steve always got low marks in English but that was more due to his general awkwardness and lack of discipline than to being weak in the subject. He said some bright things at times.

"What about?" he asked, and half expected to be blasted by a sarcastic retort. But Steve said: "Oh, just slush. Pirates in the South Seas—that sort of stuff. It's crazy, but it passes the time."

"Can I read it?"

"You can if you don't mind being bored to shreds." He stared at Marty. "You heard from Paul yet?"

"I saw him tonight when he visiphoned home."

"How is he?"

"He seemed all right."

Steve said enviously: "He's lucky."

"In a way." A thought struck Marty. "Being sent down . . . why can't you go? I mean, you don't have any folks in the Bubble."

Steve lived with foster parents who had a boy of their own, some years younger, with whom he seemed to have less in common even than with other boys. He said: "I don't have folks down below, either. Or none who wants to go to the trouble of making a claim. I'm a ward of the Colony and the Colony says I'm better off here. They ran the medical computer on me and it opted for staying. I don't get the chance to argue till I'm eighteen."

"That's tough if you want to go."

"Doesn't everyone?"

"Well, yes." He thought of his own decision, but could not bring himself to mention it. "Though it's not too bad here really."

"Could be worse," Steve agreed. "Like a character in my book. He's been captured by the Spaniards and chained to the wall for ten years in a dungeon on one of the islands of the Spanish Main. It's right by the sea and every high tide he gets flooded to the knees. He gets bread and water, thin soup twice a week, and he has to fight the rats for it. They're two feet long, nose to tail, and keep their teeth sharp gnawing through granite. He doesn't worry either. He's only got ten years to go and he doesn't have to pay taxes."

Marty laughed. "See what you mean!"

"If you're not busy right now . . ."

"I'm not."

"I thought of going out to the Wall. See if the mountains have moved any. Have a look for a Moon-bird. You want to come along?"

Marty said: "I don't mind."

Marty's mother said: "I'm glad to see you've found a new friend."

Steve had been around to the apartment for the evening. He had brought some tapes to play, of seventeenth-century music. Marty knew very little about classical music and he had been bored some of the time, but Steve was good at explaining things and telling you what to listen for. He had enjoyed it more than he expected.

He realized his mother's remark was not entirely wholehearted. She probably was glad he was not mooching aimlessly around so much but he also knew that Steve made her uneasy, as he did most people. He was polite, but he managed to give the impression to adults of being just about to bust out in some way. She would not suggest that he look for some other companion—she had said in the past what a pity it was that Steve led such a solitary life—but she was not happy about it.

Marty said: "Steve's O.K. He's so bright I don't always understand him, but I do my best to keep up."

"He's no cleverer than you," his mother said. "He's very strong-minded, though. You don't want to let him influence you too much."

They were in the tiny kitchen and she was getting the turkey ready for tomorrow's dinner. It was Thanksgiving Day. Since there were no such things as vacations for people in the Bubble and school went on the year round, all sorts of minor holidays were celebrated. Chinese New Year, for instance, though there was only one person of Chinese origin in the Colony and he had been born in Africa and had never seen China. Tomorrow, anyway, it was battery turkey and no school. On Marty's urging, permission had been obtained for Steve to join them.

His mother asked: "What time is he coming in the morning?"

"I'm picking him up," Marty said. "We're taking a crawler out."

Over the age of twelve you could take crawlers outside the Bubble if you wanted to. It was something else that was supposed to cut down the feeling of confinement. The crawlers had governors which cut the motors if you tried to take them outside an eight-mile radius from the main lock and there was radio transmission back to the control point, so no risk was involved. His mother said: "Don't be late for dinner. One o'clock prompt."

"We'll be back. Unless we find a Moon-bird."

"A what?"

Marty laughed. "One of Steve's crazy ideas. He's full of them. He has a lot of imagination."

She trussed the turkey with a spike that had done such duty hundreds of times and would go on being used for years to come. Nothing in the Bubble was thrown away while it had any useful life left in it. She said: "Some imagination's a good thing. Too much isn't. Here especially."

He knew what she was talking about. People were picked for mental stability but occasionally it broke down. Only a month ago a man had gone outside, tried (absurdly) to shatter the Bubble with a crowbar and then, with a dozen watching him from the other side of the barrier, had taken off his helmet and choked in vacuum.

"Steve's all right," Marty said.

She smiled. "I'm sure he is. Open up the refrigerator, darling, while I pop this in."

It was dull, dull. The sun's glare was harsher without the Bubble's protective tinting and there was dust and rock all around instead of the familiar paths and buildings, but there was really nothing to be seen that could not have been seen as well through one of the telescopes in the Viewing Room. The crawler lurched through a landscape that, apart from being arid and lifeless, was utterly without surprise. In the relatively near distance was the launch station; farther away the smaller dome of one of the mines. The former lay within the crawler's active radius, the latter not. A special key was needed to unlock the control that overrode the governor, and Control Section issued them only to people who were on duty. There were spacesuits in the crawler, but the same key was needed for opening the external door of the crawler's airlock.

Steve drove the crawler under the escarpment until the motor died. He said: "See that draw, just up ahead?"

Perhaps a quarter of a mile away the escarpment split, showing a channel, wide enough to take the crawler, that led obliquely upward. You could see in for fifty yards or so before it twisted and disappeared. Marty nodded.

"I see it."

"It leads up to the mountains."

"I know."

"You know what you might find up there?"

"Moon-birds?"

Steve said slowly: "Maybe a ship came down, maybe thousands of years ago. When the Egyptians were building the pyramids. Maybe they looked in on them too. A scouting expedition from Rigel or Betelgeuse. Only one of the ships crashed, here on the Moon. Nothing would change, nothing can, so it's still there. Nose crumpled, airlock burst open. So you could crawl through and see what's inside. All sorts of weird machines and instruments."

Marty said: "You wouldn't see anything. No lights. Whatever kind of power they used it wouldn't be still functioning after thousands of years."

"Maybe they built the hull out of a transparent material. Like the Bubble, only harder. Something like diamond. A diamond, half a mile long and hollow."

"Diamond's carbon. It would burn to a cinder as soon as you hit an atmosphere."

"You have a point," Steve said. "I could say that perhaps that's what did happen—perhaps the rest of the fleet burned up in the Earth's atmosphere—but that would mean the Rigelians or the Betelgeusians were pretty stupid not to work it out in advance. And diamond's brittle as well as being hard." He shook his head. "Not too probable, really."

Marty said: "Maybe the power switched off when they hit, but works again when someone comes inside. You trip a lever or something."

"Or maybe the Moon-birds have been nesting in it, and they lay these big luminous eggs." Steve pushed the control lever into reverse and the motor hummed into life. The crawler moved back and they could see the marks of its tracks in the Moondust, going so far and no farther. "I suppose we might as well head for home."

"We could go over to the launch station."

"No traffic for a week," Steve said. "I'd as soon go back inside."

Marty's father made up a bottle of white wine from instant and converted it to champagne-type by adding sparkle. The boys had a glass each with their meal. Everyone ate a lot and afterward they switched on TV. It was a revival of a remake of a musical spectacular. The adults watched it with mild somnolent interest. After a quarter of an hour the boys excused themselves and went out.

"What now?" Marty asked. "I suppose we could go along to the Center and have a game of zing."

Zing was purely local. It had evolved out of table tennis in response to the Moon's lower gravity. It had a complicated set of rules and in place of table and net a flat surface with one end contained in a sort of box and the other end open. You played from the open end into the box.

Steve said: "You beat me too easily." Games bored him and he could not stay interested after the first few minutes. "We might as well go there as anywhere, though."

They cabined to the Center, squashing together into one rather than taking two. The game rooms were full of others who were, like them, free from school and seeking ways of passing time. The kindergarten was the only place where there was room to move: since it was a holiday the little ones were home with their mothers who normally left them there while on duty. Marty and Steve fooled around with the equipment, built a castle of bricks and knocked it down. Then Steve said: "Remember this?"

He was holding a warm-air tube. It was used for heating certain low-melting-point plastics. The heat came from a fuel cell and did not get above 40° centigrade so it was quite safe even for very small children. They could use it to bend and reshape plastic rods and other objects.

Marty said: "Yes. But I was never mad on plastics modeling."

"Nor was I. It's just that I've had an idea."

"What?"

"Come on up to the storeroom. I want to see if I can find something."

The storeroom was a closely packed and organized repository of items that had a seasonal use in the Center: lanterns for the Chinese New Year, different sets of decorations, Christmas trees and streamers—all that sort of thing. It was among the Christmas stuff that Steve found what he was looking for: a carton of reusable balloons, carefully deflated and packed away for next year.

Marty said: "Well?"

"Hot air rises. If we use the warm-air tube to inflate them and let them go out of the window . . . they'll float up to the underside of the Bubble."

The idea was appealing . . . dozens of balloons bobbing upward and fastening themselves against the curved invisible roof overhead. He said: "And when the temperature equalizes . . ."

"They'll drop again, but they'll dodge about a bit in the convection currents. They should spread pretty well all over the Bubble before they're all down. There's something else too."

"What?"

"The paints downstairs in the kindergarten. We could paint faces on them before we send them up. You can draw pretty well."

"I can do Sherrin. That bushy moustache and receding hairline and those old-type spectacles." The principal of the school would not wear contact lenses, claiming they irritated his eyes. "He's pretty easy."

"Make them all Sherrin," Steve said. "Forty or fifty Sherrins floating down all over—how's that for a nightmare?"

Marty laughed. "What are we waiting for?"

Mr. Sherrin removed the old-type spectacles from his nose, and polished them with a cloth. He stared at the two boys who faced him across his desk. When he had given the forbidding silence time to sink in, he said: "Does either of you have any explanation, or excuse?"

Marty said: "No, sir." Steve echoed him a fraction later.

Mr. Sherrin said: "I would not have thought I needed to remind you of the importance of discipline in the Colony, nor of the dangers of thoughtlessness. To take the materials question first, you have wasted paint and also, unless a caricature of my features is to darken Christmas for years to come, wasted balloons. Neither of these is made here; both have to be freighted across nearly two hundred and fifty thousand miles of space. This is not trivial because on the Moon no waste is trivial.

This is something you have been taught over and over again, and which by your ages you ought to act on instinctively. Do you accept what I am saying?"

They accepted. It was all, Marty knew, absolutely right and sensible. Mr. Sherrin went on: "Waste apart, there is the question of indiscipline. I am not so much referring to poking fun at your superiors as to the indulging of a childish whim. We do not have whims on the Moon. We cannot afford them. Everyone's life in this Colony depends on discipline and co-operation, and if it is to work in large things it must be rigidly enforced in small."

He pushed his spectacles back on.

"Now," he said, "I am not going to try to allocate responsibility between you. I have a suspicion, Marty, that you may have done rather more on the artistic side, but very likely Steve made up for his deficiency there in other ways. You were in this together, and you will be punished equally and together.

"We all suffer from boredom here, and it is probably harder on young minds than older ones. We do the best we can and the Center, of course, is the focal point for that. You two found yourselves so bored that you committed a stupid prank for which you must be punished. I could give you extra work here in school, or extra duties, but I have decided on a different course. I think you must be made to realize your good fortune in having a place like the Recreation Center, so that in future you will not treat its advantages so lightly. I am therefore banning you both from using it for one month. Is that understood?"

"Yes, sir."

"Then you can go to your class. And after school you will occupy yourselves recovering the remainder of the balloons. It may be possible to paint over Marty's artwork and use them again, though that means using still more paint, of course."

He paused. "I saw them going up. Very colorful they looked. But the Moon is not the place for colorful things. Dismiss."

3

A Key to Adventure

THE PUNISHMENT WAS MORE SEVERE THAN appeared at first sight. The Recreation Center was something Marty had taken for granted all his life; he visited it every day, occasionally several times a day, for exercises or a swim, to change books, watch a movie, or just to meet other fellows and talk. For the first few days he found himself automatically planning to go there and once he actually picked up a cabin before remembering the ban. He was left with school and home—a three-room apartment—and the tiny park with the reservoir.

It was a relief that his parents at least did not go on about it. His father told him he had behaved stupidly—that in his view Mr. Sherrin had let them off very lightly—and left it at that. His mother said nothing, but changed his books for him and did her best to help him combat boredom in other ways. She talked to him a lot, and talked about the subject which had previously been avoided: her own early life on Earth. She opened up the bottom drawer of the small locker which held her personal things, and showed him old photographs which he had never seen before—photographs of her family, the family that under other circumstances would have been his.

There was one that impressed Marty more than the others. It was a photograph of a man in his fifties, broad-faced and bearded, the curly hair of the beard streaked with white. The face was strong and looked as though it could be stern, but there were laughter wrinkles at the corners of the eyes.

"Your grandfather," his mother said. "I've never shown you any of them before because . . . well, they wouldn't mean anything to you, would they? They're just photographs, not people."

"And he was an artist, a painter?" She nodded. "He made a living out of that?"

"Not really. I think his paintings were good, but they weren't popular with the critics. He sold a few, now and then, but not many. Since he died they're becoming more valuable."

"Then how did you all manage?"

"His father—your great-grandfather—was fairly rich."

Marty said: "I see."

She shook her head. "I don't think you do. There was really quite a lot of money. He gave most of it away, keeping only just enough for us. And not to live luxuriously, either. We lived in different parts of the world at different times, but usually in broken-down houses in the country and quite modestly. It was not that he was ashamed of the money, or of being a painter. He worked hard at it and he thought it was a worthwhile thing to do. But he liked living simply, and he wanted us to do the same. The money was paid once a month through the bank, and there were times we ran short before the end and had to skimp like mad. Once we lived on bread and herrings for a week. That was when we were living by the sea in Norway. And we had shabby shoes and all my clothes were handed down from my two sisters. No, there was very little in the way of luxury."

He could see that while she was talking she was remembering; her face relaxed from its anxious lines into a smile. Marty asked: "When did he die?"

She hesitated and the smile went. "After we came up here. A couple of years before you were born."

"What was he like?"

"It's difficult to say. A hard man, in some ways. It was hopeless to try to argue with him when his mind was made up. And yet very gentle. Birds and animals did not seem to be frightened of him—he used to tame them wherever we went. And he had this tremendous sense of humor. He was always either terribly serious or making people laugh."

The smile had crept back. She went on talking about him, and Marty listened. He could see how happy she had been as a girl, and it made it worse that she was so much less happy now. This life, confining for all, was harder on her because of the freedom she had known. He asked her what his grandfather had thought about her decision to come to the Moon Colony, and she was evasive and sad. He did not press the point on her. There was no need to. It was very obvious what the big bearded man, the artist and the wanderer, would have felt about such a limited and colorless existence.

He felt a sudden resentment against his father, who took the Bubble for granted, who was neither particularly serious nor humorous, whom it was difficult to imagine taming birds and animals even if one could imagine birds and animals being here. Above all, who was responsible for his mother being here instead of leading the life she really wanted— since plainly it was only because of his father that she had chosen to come.

Marty had seen very little of Steve since the interview with Mr. Sherrin. He had been asked to visit a lot, to homes where there was a boy of around his age, and his mother encouraged him to ask them back and put on special treats when he did so. Then

one day he accidentally overheard a visiphone conversation between her and another mother, Mrs.
Parker, which explained things. It was clear from
what Mrs. Parker was saying that there was a general
attempt being made to detach him from what was
thought to be Steve's bad influence. The old doubts
and reservations about Steve had given rise to the
conviction that he had been responsible for what
had happened—that he had talked Marty into it.

What brought Marty up short and made him
particularly indignant was the fact that he had held
a similar sort of view himself. He had been annoyed
with Steve for helping to get him into trouble and
very much aware of the idea having been Steve's in
the first place. He realized he had been, to some
extent, avoiding him.

That other people thought the same, that this
was taken for granted in the Bubble, showed him
the injustice of it. Even if the notion had been
Steve's he had more than cooperated. After all, he
had painted the faces on the balloons. And Steve,
who had been friendless in the first place, was being
further isolated while he was having people make

things easy for him. He waited until his mother had gone to the store and dialed Steve's home. Steve himself answered, his face coalescing out of the blur of the screen.

Marty said: "Hi. How are things with you?"

"I've known them brighter. You?"

"The same. I wondered if you might be drifting up toward the park."

"Now?"

"Unless you're busy."

It had occurred to him while he was talking that Steve might well be feeling some resentment over the way he had neglected him lately. He showed no sign of it, though. He laughed.

"Busy doing nothing. I'll see you there."

They met and talked; about nothing much but he felt better afterward. When he got back his mother asked him where he had been, and he told her. A little later she asked him if he were going over to Ben Trillici's as he had planned.

Marty shook his head. "I'm going to Steve's."

"But hadn't you fixed things with Ben?"

"No. It wasn't fixed. I said I might drop around."

"Don't you think you would be letting him down if you don't go?"

"He has a couple of other guys coming. If I'm not there they can go up to the Center if they feel like it—have a game of zing. Otherwise they have to stick with me and get bored."

She sighed, but did not dispute this. Marty said: "O.K. if I ask Steve along tomorrow?"

"Of course. If you want to."

"I do."

It was Steve's suggestion, a couple of days later, that they should take a crawler out again. The rocket from Earth was due in, and it was true, as he said, that you got a better view of the landing from outside. Not that this would normally have been such an overwhelming attraction—it was a sight almost as familiar as the sun's rays breaking through the gaps in the easterly mountains for the lunar dawn—but in present circumstances filling in time had become important. Mr. Sherrin's intention of making them appreciate the advantages of the Center was being fulfilled very effectively.

There were five crawlers at the service bay just inside the main airlock. Steve was for taking the first one, but Marty, on impulse, decided to look along the rank. Steve asked what was the point in doing that—the crawlers were identical, after all— but shrugged and followed.

The crawler at the end was out of line with the others, as though whoever brought it in last had been in a hurry to get back home. They climbed in and Marty stared at the control panel. He had been in a hurry, all right, or else careless. He had left the key in its slot. Silently he nudged Steve, who had come in behind him.

There was a pause before Steve said: "I used to come here hoping for that one time. I'd given up, though." He pulled the key out and slipped it back in. "It's real."

"What do you think?"

"There's nothing in the rules. I mean, it says you have to apply for a key and we know we wouldn't get one, but there's nothing about finding one in a crawler. We could even not have noticed it till we were outside the Bubble. What do you say we haven't noticed it?"

"Are we going to use it, though?"

"Do we have to decide right now? But if we went the same way we went last time—another few hundred yards and we could at least have a look what it's like up that draw."

"Yes." Marty felt a rising excitement; out of proportion really with the proposition Steve had put forward. "Let's move then. Before he remembers he didn't take the key out, and comes back."

He himself took the controls. He pressed the port-closing button and the airlock doors closed. Then he put the drive in forward and the crawler began to move.

His flashing light, showing that he was going outside, was answered by a wink from the box and the inner wall of the main airlock lifted for them. Marty drove forward and then had to wait while that wall came down, the precious air was sucked out, and the outer wall opened to the vacuum. His nerves prickled with the thought that at any moment the man who had left the key would return—that the lifting wall-section would drop again, the radio order them in. But nothing happened. He pushed the lever back to forward and the crawler trundled out onto the black basalt rock surrounding the Bubble.

They reached the point where the governor cut in and stopped the motor. Marty and Steve looked at each other.

"They haven't called us," Steve said. "Even if anyone contacted us they couldn't tell where we were, within a quarter mile."

Behind them they could see the Bubble, or at any rate the top of the dome and the wireless mast. Level horizons on the Moon were only two miles distant and the base was lost behind the curve. Marty turned the key. The motor hummed into life again, and the crawler lurched forward.

They did not speak until they were in sight of the draw which had fascinated Steve. It was a great disappointment. It ran up steeply for some fifty yards and petered out at a sheer rock face. Steve said: "I've always thought this was the pass that goes up through the mountains."

Marty went back to the realization that people were trying to cut him off from Steve. It was not only that he had thought it unjust. There had been a little resentment as well at their assumption that the balloon stunt had been all Steve's idea—that he did not have the initiative, or maybe the nerve, to do something like that unless he were dragged into it. He said: "Have you looked in the store locker?"

"Yes. It's full. That last trip must have been a very short one. If it had been refilled, someone would have been bound to spot the key." Steve ran a hand through his black wiry hair. "Why?"

"That pass. It must be somewhere along here. It cuts across the foothills of the main range. First Station is on the plain beyond them. That's not much more than three hundred miles. We could get there in a couple of days."

Steve said: "It means trouble. We might get away with having used the key. Even with scouting a bit farther along. But if we're away for nearly a week . . ."

The trouble it meant scarcely bore thinking about. They would have everyone on top of them.

Marty felt a slight trembling at the knees. He would not be too sorry if Steve vetoed the plan. He shrugged and said: "Just as you like."

"But we'll never get a chance like this again." Steve examined the reading on the oxygen tank. "Almost full. That gives us fourteen days clear." He looked up. "I'm game if you are."

"O.K." Marty hoped his voice sounded steadier than it felt. "Then let's get going. Before they realize we're out here and haul us back."

"There's one thing."

"What's that?"

"We don't want to have them mount a search for us."

"No." The thought was appalling: all the resources of the colony marshaled in a hunt whose cost was scarcely computable. One might waste paint and balloons, but expense of this order was unthinkable to a Lunarian. "In that case . . ."

"We can drop a beacon."

He meant a radio beacon. They were carried as part of the crawler's emergency equipment and consisted of transmitters linked to miniature tape recorders and time clocks. When set, a message was beamed out at regular intervals.

"They'll pick it up right away," Marty objected. "And with a jumbo crawler they can catch us in ten minutes. Five, more likely."

"Set the clock for delayed transmission. An hour, say. By that time we'll be well out of reach, especially if we're up in the foothills."

This was true. Marty searched his mind for other objections and found none: none, that was, except the trouble they would be in when they got back. Overhead was the pale crescent of Earth, to the east the harsh orb of the sun, twenty-four hours risen. The fuel cells which powered the crawler were even now being replenished with energy from the battery of photoelectric cells on the roof. A journey through the mountains meant a considerable time spent in shadow, but with the sun rising toward its zenith there would be plenty of opportunity for finding patches of sunlight in which they could recharge. They had over twelve days before lunar night fell, more than twice as long as they would need.

Steve said: "I'll record the message."

Marty guessed his hesitation had been inter-preted as reluctance. If the message were in Steve's voice it could seem that Steve was chiefly responsible. He said hotly: "No. This was my idea."

Steve shrugged. "As you like. Not that it makes much difference. We're both for it when we get back. Better not say we're heading for First Station. They might send a hopper over and be waiting for us."

Marty nodded. He picked up the recorder, flicked the switch, and spoke into the tiny micro-phone: "This is Marty, Marty Collins. We took out this crawler—it's number . . . 217—and we found it had a key left in. I've overridden the governor and we're going to explore for a few days. Steve du Cros is with me. We've checked provisions, air and power. Everything is O.K. We're just going to hunt around. We'll be back before nightfall. Would you tell Mr. Sherrin, please, that any work we miss at school we'll make up when we come back? I'm tim-ing this to transmit an hour after recording, so don't bother to try looking for us. We're really all right. Signing off now."

Steve handed him the metal sphere of the beacon and he slotted the tape spool into place. He checked for transmission and then, consulting his finger-watch, set the time. He dropped the sphere into the shaft of the small disposal lock, buttoned the air out into the crawler's general supply, and pressed the button which opened the other end. The sphere came into view in the side observation window, rolling down a slight slope. It stopped after a few yards.

"Ready to move?" he asked Steve.

The palms of his hands were sweating despite the air-conditioned atmosphere. He rubbed them surreptitiously on his trousers.

"Sure," Steve said. "You want to carry on driving?"

"We could do the usual shifts."

They knew the routine for two-man crawlers on extended patrols. Two hours on duty, two off, for eight hours, followed by two six-hour shifts to enable the person not driving to get some sleep in the bunk that was built into one wall.

Steve nodded. "I'll start by map-reading, then."

Not long afterward the Earth rocket flashed in the sky, settling on its flame-tail into the launch basin. They paid no attention to it.

The pass they wanted was less than half a mile farther on, past a jutting spur of rock that was clearly marked on the map. Steering the crawler up into it, Marty had a last glimpse of the Bubble behind them, its top gleaming in the sunlight. His nervousness had left him through having to concentrate on driving. He had previously only handled crawlers on the more or less flat plateau around the Bubble and the incline before them was steep in places. The tracks bit well enough to begin with, but farther on there was a place where they could not get sufficient purchase and the crawler slipped and skidded backward. He engaged the climbing spikes and tried again. This time, with the sharp steel claws emerging from the tracks to grip and hold the rock, it went up with no difficulty. The slope flattened again and he retracted the spikes. Their points were of specially hardened steel, but it was important to avoid unnecessary wear on them.

The sun not being very high, they lost it almost at once in the narrow defile through which they were climbing. Marty drove by light reflected from the dazzling walls of sunlit rock high above them. The crawlers were fitted with powerful headlight beams but he did not need to use them. Beside him Steve followed their course on the map.

"Looks straightforward," he said. "We're definitely heading the right way. That zigzag followed by a right-angled turn . . . and the pass broadens out just ahead."

"What comes after?"

"You take the left fork half a mile on. Then it's fairly straight for something like ten miles. But the contour lines are close—you may need spikes."

They sat side by side in silence, watching the walls close in and then recede. Straightforward, certainly. Maybe dull in due course, but for the moment there was novelty in it, a pleasant tension, a feeling that each new vista might reveal something strange. And where the pass broadened to a valley wide enough and at the right angle for the sun's rays to penetrate, it did. Steve drew Marty's attention to a gleam of metal away to the right. He headed the crawler that way. It was impossible that they could have chanced on something unknown, of course— the route was marked on the map and had been traveled probably hundreds of times already—but there was a tingle of anticipation all the same.

A moment later he recognized the metal for what it was: a broken and discarded rock drill. Someone had been taking samples here. The rock face showed core holes in a number of places. There were other signs of activity, including several empty food containers. Seeing them reminded Marty that several hours had elapsed since breakfast. He mentioned this to Steve, who said: "Yes. And I guess I'm cook. What would you like? Moon-rabbit roasted on a spit, with baked potatoes? Or how about a nice fresh lunar salmon, cooked in the hot embers of a campfire? Pull over to the nearest stream and I'll see what I can do."

Rabbit and salmon came into the very long list of things known through TV and through TV only. Potatoes were grown in the Bubble but were treats for special occasions: there were more economical ways of producing starch.

Steve rummaged in the food locker and came up with two cans.

"Or would you like minced chicken mush with artificial flavoring? Because that's what you're going to get." He pulled the tag to operate the chemical heater. "But done to a turn, I promise you that."

"Sounds great," Marty said.

"We can even have music with it. The last time I looked it was the Pacific facing us up there. We could try for some of that Oriental jazz from Tokyo."

He switched the radio on and began searching the dial. He found a couple of weak stations, talking, and a still weaker one playing music through a barrier of static. Then he said: "I suppose we could check the service channel. See if they're calling us to come back yet."

He clicked in to the Control frequency. There was no direct radio communication beyond the very short horizon range but the orbiting satellites circling the Moon picked up signals and bounced them back. Someone was talking to a crawler heading for the mines, a routine message. Steve said: "Either they've not missed us or they're not bothered. I suppose we could leave it on this channel?"

There had been a sick feeling in the pit of Marty's stomach which was only slightly subsiding as the even, routine voice on the radio continued to talk. It was one thing to evade regulations, quite another to defy an order openly.

He said: "Do we have to?"

"No," Steve said. He switched off. "I don't suppose we do. I think those barbecued steaks must be about ready."

4

First Station

WHEN STEVE TOOK OVER DRIVING, MARTY was able to study the map at leisure. You could read it while you were driving, but only really effectively by means of the map screen which picked out and illuminated a sector at a time according to the way you moved the wind knob. In fact they had not bothered to put it through the screen; Steve had kept it spread out on a table.

It was as simple as Steve had said. From the small circle marking the Bubble it was easy to trace their route up through the foothills to their present position, and as easy to follow it onward to the point where it doglegged between two peaks and stood over above the plain and the cross marking First Station. The last bit was through a warren of cross-hatchings which could have been confusing except that they would be on the short run down to their destination: any downward path took one to the plain from which one would see the dome of the station. The descent was shown as steep: they would need the spikes for braking. Not that it would matter if the crawler did lose adhesion and slid down. These vehicles were toughly built and well sprung to cope with minor impacts.

Simple, but slow. On a level, easy surface a crawler could make fifteen or twenty miles an hour. In terrain like the present a third of that would be good going. They were two hours on their way, out of something like fifty. There were going to be dull patches during that time.

They settled into a routine, taking turns on the controls and the map. After eight hours there was the first rest period. Steve proposed throwing dice for who slept first but Marty insisted that, having taken the first short stint, he must also take the first long one. Steve did not argue but yawned and crawled into the bunk, zipping the curtain which ran the full length and left him in a soundproofed and specially padded cocoon. The alarm was set to waken him in six hours. During that period Marty was on his own.

They were high, but still climbing. The crawler was heading along a fairly straight defile with the sun hidden but the Earth a luminous crescent almost centrally above. The part he could see appeared to be covered with cloud. He wondered what it must be like—those short days that started, perhaps, in sunshine . . . and then the sun being hidden, rain falling. He had seen it, of course, on films but that wasn't like feeling it. Feeling rain, for instance . . . drops of water, millions of them, falling out of the sky.

It was all there, above him but a quarter of a million miles away. The thought of that distance, normally taken for granted, was suddenly overpowering. He was contemplating it not from the familiar confines of the Bubble but through the observation panel of this tiny, lurching machine, making its staggering way through mountains that had never known cloud or rain, for thousands on thousands of years.

He switched on the radio for company and found a fairly strong station playing what he recognized as some kind of opera. It lasted for a quarter of an hour before fading. He searched for another, but could not find one worth listening to. They were all so tiny and distorted that the sound merely emphasized his isolation. He let his fingers rest on the switch that would put the set on Control frequency. He had a great urge to hear a voice he knew. But if the voice were ordering him to turn the crawler around and come back? The thought made him feel a little weak at the knees. He snapped the radio off, and concentrated on the track in front of him.

Gradually he grew more accustomed to being alone. Halfway through the shift he took a hot drink and a packet of concentrate-cookies and, making another search for Earth stations, found one that was strong and fairly steady. A man with an accent which Marty recognized as Australian was giving a cricket commentary. Lunarians had no interest in games that took up large areas of space and he knew nothing at all about cricket, but it was comforting to listen to.

"McAndrew is coming up to bowl, slow left hand, round the wicket . . . he tosses it right up and Barlow takes it on his pads, outside the leg stump. It runs away and Janutschek comes in from short square leg to pick it up. That's the end of the over, taking the England score to five for a hundred and nine, and yes, I think there's going to be an appeal against the light. The umpires are consulting. But they're not coming in. Shelton has the ball to bowl from the Pavilion end. He's marking out his run now . . . thirteen, fourteen, fifteen, sixteen paces. Pinkard takes guard. Shelton is coming in to bowl . . ."

An appeal against the light presumably meant that a cloud was so darkening the sky that the batsmen might not be able to see the ball properly. The crawler came out onto a wide shelf of rock and abruptly was in sunshine. It dazzled Marty's eyes until he buttoned the dimming blind into position.

At the end of six hours the bell pinged on both sides of the bunk curtain and a few moments later Steve emerged, rubbing his eyes. Marty showed him their position on the map, told him there was nothing to report, and took his place in the bunk. He zipped the curtain, snapped out the light, and stretched out exhausted on the mattress. The springs and foam padding beneath him converted the jolting of the crawler into a gentle soporific rocking. Not, he felt as he drifted into sleep, that he needed any rocking. His eyes ached from the strain of watching the trail of rock unfold. He could not remember ever feeling so tired.

He came awake gradually and was surprised to find that he was lying in darkness. He could not recall hearing the alarm, and anyway it should have automatically put the light on. Had he woken up before time? Yet he felt fully refreshed.

He found and pressed the light switch and looked at his finger-watch. Nearly a quarter past eight. The alarm had been set for six. Did that mean that something had gone wrong . . . ? The tracker was in motion though, steadily lurching along. Marty unzipped the curtain and tumbled out into the cabin.

Steve turned from the controls and said: "Hi."

"The alarm didn't work. You should have called me." He saw the alarm switch on the cabin side; it was in the off position. "That was set when I went to bed. Did you turn it off?"

"I thought you might as well have your sleep out. You looked beat."

He knew it was unreasonable, but felt angry. Steve showing his superiority: he could make out on the six-hour bunk time that was standard on patrols but Marty was presumed not to be up to it. He said sharply: "Why was I supposed to be any more beat than you?"

"You'd been awake six hours longer, hadn't you? You insisted on taking the first long shift."

That was true enough. His anger cooled, but left some resentment. He said: "Don't do it again without telling me. All right?"

Steve grinned. "As you like, skipper. How do you feel about making us some breakfast? Sunny-side eggs and crisp grilled bacon. It's the can in the corner on the right."

Marty went to the food locker. He asked: "Anything interesting happen?"

"What could?"

• • •

Their course wound on through the foothills. As the sun slowly rose in the sky they were in harsh sunlight more of the time, which meant having to use the dimming blind but also meant that the batteries were kept at full charge. For the most part they saw only the walls of the valley or ravine through which the crawler was traveling, but occasionally there were glimpses of the high dazzling peaks of the mountains and once, from an eminence, a view of the Sea of Rains behind them, though not of the Bubble. They made one error by taking a wrong path into a cul-de-sac which stopped them dead after twenty minutes. Marty was at the wheel, Steve navigating. The crawler faced a wall of rock in which, Steve pointed out, there were gleaming flecks of something that was not ordinary stone.

"Gold?" Marty asked.

"False gold, more likely. But it might be worth making a note of it."

If they were able to report an important new site for mining, Marty thought, the authorities might go a little easier on them. The crawler backed up to the point which he recognized as the one where they had gone wrong, and he stopped fooling himself. Nothing was going to get them out of trouble when they went back to the Bubble. The best thing to do was not dwell on it.

They had crossed the spine of the foothills and were descending by the time Steve went into the bunk again. The descent was not a steady one, of course—there were twists and backtrackings and occasional quite steep climbs—but on the whole they were heading downward and he was using the spikes from time to time to prevent a slide. Marty did not find the loneliness quite so overpowering this time, and the shift went reasonably quickly. At the end of six hours Steve reappeared and Marty took his place. He was very tired again and dropped off right away. The alarm woke him, and he came out to find the crawler heading along a dark and narrow canyon that dropped steeply in front of them. The walls were so close overhead that it was almost like being in a tunnel, and Steve had the headlights on to see his way.

It was tricky terrain, as Marty discovered when he took over. Both lights and grip-spikes had to be used frequently, and however much care one took it was impossible to prevent the crawler's treads occasionally losing adhesion and the crawler itself suddenly sliding, throwing the pair of them against one or another of the padded interior surfaces. Toward the end of this shift they came out into a broader valley where the slope looked moderate but, as he increased power, they were unexpectedly on scree. The crawler slithered for fifty yards before smacking up against a rock face. It gave them quite a shaking.

Journey's end, when it came, was unexpected. Marty steered the crawler around a rubble slope and the sunshine was blinding ahead of them, reflected not off a few peaks or high walls but from the great plain ahead. He blinked, his eyes adjusting to the brilliance, and caught the gleam of something that was not rock but man-made and symmetrical—the small Bubble, no more than twenty yards across, of First Station.

The suits were too big, but since they were designed to fit men of differing physiques it was possible to wear them without much difficulty or discomfort. They went through the crawler's airlock and stood for a few moments in the shade of the vehicle before proceeding. It was not the first time Marty had been in a spacesuit—children were trained to use them in vacuum as part of the Bubble's safety program—but he felt different about this. Steve was silent beside him, for so long that Marty wondered if anything was wrong. Then he realized that he had not switched the suit radio on, and did so. Steve was saying: "... go right in? Or scout around it first?"

The station's airlock was in front of them, and open. There had been no point in closing it when it was abandoned: no wind or weather could affect it. He felt a reluctance, and said: "Let's look around."

The perimeter was only a little over a hundred yards in extent, which they could cover in a few minutes in float jumps. On the second, though, they halted. They stared together at the cairn of boulders, very bright in the sunlight, and the metal post in front of it with the small plaque on top. It had four names on it, the names of the men who had died here at First Station. Three of them lay beneath the cairn, in graves blasted out of the rock. Their bodies would be as they had been at the moment of death. Decay and corruption were signs of life, and the Moon was lifeless. Mullins, Anquetil, Sharp. Marty looked at the fourth name. "Andrew Thurgood, not recovered." He knew the story, from the books about First Station and the feature film that was still shown occasionally. Thurgood was the one who had taken out a crawler and not come back. They had searched for him, but found nothing. He was supposed to have said strange things before he went. It was guessed that his mind had been turned by the stress of living on the Moon, that he had traveled on until the batteries of his crawler were drained, his food and oxygen used up, and had died in some remote corner of one of the hundreds of thousands of clefts and gulches which covered the Moon's surface.

"What made them come here?" Steve asked. "What made anyone come here?"

It was a question that was never asked, one from which the mind rebelled. Marty thought of Paul, wondering what he was doing now. Out of the rehabilitation center, maybe, walking in fields somewhere, smelling flowers, feeling the wind against his face. He stared at the changeless scene in front of him.

"Let's go inside," he said. "There's nothing to see out here."

They jump-floated back to the entrance and went in. It was a cramped maze of catwalks and constructions, familiar from the feature film and yet utterly strange. It had been left, when it was abandoned for the Bubble, which was put up on the new and better site on the other side of the range, as a relic, a museum, and he had had the idea that it would look like the pictures of museums on Earth, with everything properly set out and labeled. Instead there was clutter, the clutter, almost, of a place that people had just left and would soon be coming back to.

Anything of value, of course, had been taken—anything that could be used. But what remained was much more than the bare bones, the basic structures. In a garbage sack hanging from its wall hook there were empty cans and cartons, left from the preparation of the last meal eaten here. The tomato sauce and solitary bean at the bottom of one of the cans had frozen and thawed again each fourteen-day cycle over more than half a century but, since there were no bacteria, had not changed in all that time. On the floor Marty saw a chewing-gum wrapper and a plastic button. Steve was picking something up from one corner. He said through the radio: "What's that?"

Steve's voice buzzed back at him. "A camera. Why would they leave that? I get it. It's broken. Smashed, in fact. Not only the lens; the casing as well."

"That bit in the film," Marty said, "where Anquetil saved Stenberg when he slipped down that fissure— didn't he drop his camera? I suppose they brought it back, and then realized it was beyond mending."

Steve turned the camera over in his hands. "Could be. Something has certainly hit it hard at some time."

"The drop was more than fifty yards."

Steve said: "You know all that stuff, don't you?"

"Well, don't you?"

Steve nodded. "Like I know the cabin route between the apartment and school. I wouldn't say it stirs the imagination."

Marty left him and climbed a catwalk to the top chamber, the observatory. The telescope they had used was still there. He looked through the eyepiece without moving it and saw, as he had guessed would be the case, that it was trained on the distant Earth. Latitude around 40° North; at the moment the hazy coastline of Japan but that was the latitude of part of the United States, too. Someone perhaps taking a last look at home before the move-out.

Leaving First Station as it was had not been merely a sentimental gesture. Even then the priorities of lunar life had been clear. No waste, no needless effort. A lot of the structures could have been dismantled and shifted, but the energy consumption would have been too high. The telescope . . . probably that would have been taken except that the Genevascope had come in around that time and rendered old-fashioned optical instruments obsolete.

The sleeping quarters were below ground level. Light switches and fittings were in place and undamaged but there was no power. Marty could hear Steve moving around somewhere but could not see him. He activated his suit-lamp, broadening the beam to diffuse the light. There were the bunks, a table, shelves. No books—they would have been taken—but some pinups on the walls. Girls mostly, but some of landscapes—a slanting meadow with belled cows beneath a dazzling slope of snow, a seacoast with twisted ocher rocks and a fantastic gray overhanging wave. And on one of the shelves a photograph wallet which, opened, showed on one side a woman, smiling under a big summer hat, on the other a big black dog with a boy beside him. The boy was about three, dressed in shorts and shirts out of a historical film. He wondered why the photograph had been abandoned and realized it was probably because it had belonged to one of the men who lay outside under the cairn. Seventy years ago. The boy would be an old man now, if he were still alive.

He lay on one of the bunks, staring at the ceiling which pressed close down on him. It was no worse than sleeping in a crawler bunk but that was for a few nights, a week maybe. Three years had been the shortest time any of the early colonists had spent here.

The bunk was of metal, enclosing broad strips of intertwined plastic, much less resilient than the kind they used now. It had been bolted to the wall and there was a small gap, no more than half an inch, at the side. He twisted around, getting up, and the beam from his suit-lamp lit it for a moment and showed something there. He peered and could distinguish it better. A thin book? He pulled the side of the bunk but it was immovable. It was impossible to get at it with his spacesuited fingers; even without the awkwardness of mittens the gap would have been too small. It could not be anything important, anyway. He left the bunk, abandoning it, and then found himself drawn back. He studied the crack more closely. If one could get something long and thin, it might be possible to hook it out.

The bunks had angle irons reinforcing their corners, strips of steel some eight by three quarter inches. He got one off, using the screwdriver attachment of the multi-tool on his belt. Then he began the fishing operation. It was not easy. Once he thought he had got the book, only to have it slip even farther down. He almost abandoned the idea—the strip of metal was awkward to use and he felt himself sweating inside the suit. It would be good to get back in the crawler and rub a cleansing pad over himself. He decided he would make one more effort, and when that failed gave himself an absolutely final one. It was two attempts after that before he managed to get the steel firmly under the object, and lifted it clear.

It was a notebook, the leaves paper and not plastic. He fumbled it open and saw that it was in the nature of a log or journal. There was an entry:

"Day 402. Crawler duty with Barney. Nothing to report. At least he doesn't talk all the time like Mike. Got back to find that stupid argument about the weight of a seagull still going on. Everyone talking, even Lew in it now. They could settle it in a few minutes by sending a signal back requesting information, but I suppose they think that would cause alarm or something. And they don't want to settle it anyway. If they did, there would be nothing to argue about. My weight today 167 lbs.—minus one. Due for a haircut, but can't be bothered to fix it with Barney."

He flipped the pages and read a couple more entries, which seemed as dull and trivial as the first. He thought of leaving the journal here, where it belonged, and then decided Steve might like to look at it. He wedged it into his suit-pouch, and started up the ladder.

Steve's radio came through to him as he reached

ground level: ". . . you've got to. Marty?"

"I'm here," he said. "I've been down below."

"Anything there?"

"Nothing much. You find anything?"

"Only lumber."

"We could give it a rest for now. I could do with a rub-down."

Steve nodded, awkwardly in the suit. "A drink, too. Let's go."

They left the station and headed for the nearby crawler. Steve went through the airlocks first, and Marty waited impatiently for him to be clear. Then it was his turn. He tugged his suit open, with relief, as soon as the inner door closed. Steve was already at the food locker, getting a couple of drink capsules. He handed Marty one, and snapped open the top of the other. He drank deeply and said: "That's good."

He did not look happy, though. While Marty drank his, more slowly, he stared out of the front observation port at the dome of the station.

"We made it," he said. His voice was flat. "All the way from nowhere to nowhere. Was it worth it, do you think?"

5

The Impossible Flower

THEY WERE BOTH DEPRESSED AND BORED. They sat in the crawler, Steve in the driving seat and Marty on the edge of the bunk, and tried to think of something to do. Through the window Marty could see First Station, the object of their adventure. He did not know what he had been hoping for but whatever it was he had not found it. It had been absurd to think there could be anything worth finding. The only difference between the Bubble and First Station was that the latter was smaller, more cramped, more primitive. It was inevitable that this should be so: the Moon with its harshness and changelessness imposed these conditions on anyone who came to live here.

He felt a wave of misery and nostalgia. It would be wonderful to push open the door of the apartment and see his mother smile in welcome, smell her cooking from the kitchen. She would be worrying about him, he realized, and felt more miserable still. They had been crazy to do it.

He said: "You seen enough?"

Steve shrugged. "Guess so."

"Shall we start back? We might as well."

"I suppose. We ought to let the batteries charge first."

This was true. The batteries had run down during their passage through the foothills; not excessively but it was standard procedure to charge up to full before going back into shadow areas. Marty got up and examined the dial. The reading was 82. It would take the photoelectric cells about an hour, he calculated, to bring it up to 100. He thought of suggesting a game of chess but that was something else in which Steve lost interest after the first few minutes. He remembered the journal he had found and pulled it out of the pouch of his discarded spacesuit.

Steve asked: "What's that?"

"A book I found in there."

"Interesting?"

The writing was very neat and even, a meticulous and dull record of routine events. Weight recorded day by day, converted to Earth poundages. It was depressing to read it; just a further confirmation of the hopelessness of expecting anything exciting to happen here. Marty threw it across to Steve.

"Have a look if you want to. I think I'll set up a problem."

It was a mate-in-four which he had been puzzling over for some time. He thought he saw a way in but it proved a blind alley. The white knight, he was sure, was the key to the solution. He checked over its possible moves with increasing exasperation.

Steve said: "I wonder who wrote this."

"Could have been anyone. Does it matter?"

"There's an odd piece here. Listen. 'Crawler patrol with Mike. Twenty-four hours.' They must have been still working on the Earth day for patrols then. He goes on: 'It was during his bunk period that I saw it. Or thought I saw it. We came through difficult high ground at 217-092, and I put her through a cleft between two peaks. Then there was high rock on the left, fissured in places. I was concentrating on the terrain immediately ahead because the going was still very tricky, and so I only caught a glimpse. Because everything is so static and unchanging here, any kind of movement attracts attention. I saw it out of the corner of my eye and looked around. It had been visible through one of the side fissures and we were almost past it. I thought I saw it, and I thought I recognized it.'"

"What was it?" Marty asked. "One of your Moon-birds?"

Steve went on reading: "'I woke Mike and told him. He thought it was a stunt—that I was getting back at him for that stupid business on my birthday. I didn't tell him what I thought it was at first—only that there had been movement, and I was applying the rule of alerting the second crew member in the event of any unusual occurrence. We backtracked to the fissure, but there was nothing to be seen. I decided to circle around and get on higher ground on the other side. The going was very tough and within half an hour we broke a track and had to go outside and repair it. Mike was fed up by this time. We finally got to a position from which we should have been looking down on the place where I had seen it, and there was still nothing. That was when Mike started pressing me on just what I had seen. What kind of movement? Falling rocks, maybe? Rocks do fall from time to time. Or volcanic activity. In the end I told him it was nothing like that. What it had looked like was a flower.'"

Marty said: "A *flower?* But that's crazy. And anyway, he said he saw it through an opening in high ground. You wouldn't have even seen anything small at that distance, let alone see it move. And flowers don't move, unless the wind blows them. He's not trying to say there was a wind on the Moon, is he?"

"Listen," Steve said. "He goes on: 'Mike laughed. He thought I was joking. He asked what kind of flower—the kind he would have liked would have been a cauliflower, done with a really rich cheese sauce. Then he started to get mad again, saying a joke was a joke but this was carrying it too far—he was missing sack time. Later still, when he realized I was serious, I could see he was becoming anxious. There's always been this talk about people going off their heads here though no one has: we were double-checked for stability before being accepted for the expedition. I wanted to enter it in the log, but he talked me out of that. It had been a trick of the light, a minor hallucination. He said "minor" but he was still anxious. I didn't press things about the log—I could tell already that it was no use— and told him to go back to sleep and I would take the crawler in. He wouldn't do that: said he was awake now and didn't need any more sleep. He was nervous on the way back. He talked a lot, as he always does, but it was all jerky, forcing things. He said no more about what I had seen, and did not refer to it when we got back to the station.'"

Steve stopped reading. Marty said: "Go on. What happened after that?"

"I'm skimming through. There's a lot of routine stuff. Bits where he comes back to it, though. Like this: 'If I did see a flower, it must have been yards across, on a stalk four or five times as long. Considered like that, it does seem nonsense. But the more I think about it, the more certain it grows in my mind. Maybe not a flower—how could it be, on the airless, waterless Moon?—but something that was capable of *resembling* a flower. Not a hallucination. I wish I had insisted on it going in the log, but I suppose in a way he was right. I think he may have said something to Lew, who has been paying more attention to me lately, asking me questions. When I came into the bunk room yesterday I had the feeling that the subject of conversation had been changed suddenly—there was a pause for a moment and then two of them started talking at once.'"

He stopped, turned over a page, and then more.

"Nothing more about it. Just routine stuff again. And that's the end. Wait a minute, though. There's this last entry: 'Lew told me this morning that I'm not to go back on patrol work tomorrow as scheduled. He was embarrassed about it, and did his best to be nice. Said we were all subject to nervous strain here, he too, and he had to work out what was best for the expedition as a whole. I did not argue; there would have been no point. But I've been thinking about it a lot, and I know I did see *something,* and something that moved. And it looked like a gigantic flower. I'd been hoping to get back to that region and explore it properly, while whoever was with me was asleep. I suppose Lew guessed this, or maybe thought I was unbalanced and a risk on that account. The thing is, we have more than another year to stick out before we go back. That's a long time to have people looking sideways at you. Whereas if I can establish that there really is something there, bring back proof . . . I'm on duty with Mike and Benny next. They've got this craze for playing cribbage. I can get out without them noticing, and the crawler's ready and stocked. I'll come back with *proof.* They won't be able to deny it then.'"

Steve looked up. "That's the end."

Marty said: "That journal . . . it must have been written by Andrew Thurgood. The one who's listed as 'not recovered.'"

"Well, obviously," Steve said. "Didn't you realize?"

"They didn't say anything in the books about flowers or anything—only about him taking a crawler without authorization and not coming back."

"I suppose Lewin McInnes didn't put it in his log, either. The accounts do say Thurgood was behaving queerly."

"A giant flower." Marty shook his head. "I suppose he went on looking for it till it was too late to get back. He wouldn't want to admit the others had been right."

"If they were right."

"What else? He must have been mad."

"He doesn't *sound* mad. Everything's very matter-of-fact apart from the flower bit. And where he's considering the possibility of it being a hallucination—that doesn't read like someone who's out of his mind."

"All right. Maybe he found the flower. A Moon-flower. Maybe he climbed up it and found a land full of Moon-giants. He didn't come back, did he? Even if he got lost, he could have radioed for help. But he didn't call them at all. Would a sane man let himself die rather than admit he was wrong?"

"I don't know," Steve said. "We could check, though."

"How do you mean, check? Check what? It was more than seventy years ago."

"The grid hasn't changed." He leafed back through the pages of the journal, looking for something. "I thought so: he gives the positional co-ordinates. 217-092. We can go and have a look."

"Have a look for what? The flower?"

"Maybe. Or Thurgood's crawler. He's bound to have headed back there."

"You're joking, aren't you?" Marty said.

"Joking? No. Maybe something went wrong with his radio—those early sets were always going on the blink."

"I'm talking about us. You weren't serious about going up there to look for him?"

"Why not?"

Marty took a deep breath. "Because I reckon it's time we headed back for the Bubble. We're in trouble enough as it is, and my guess is that the longer we stay away the worse it's going to be."

"That's one way of looking at it," Steve said. He was very calm and assured. "Or you could say that since we already are in deep trouble it can hardly be much worse."

"It's been a waste of time coming here."

"I don't know." Steve held the book up. "You found this."

"That won't help us much," Marty said bitterly. "One or two historians on Earth may find it interesting but I don't think Mr. Sherrin is likely to think it justifies anything."

"But if Thurgood was right—if there really is something funny there and we find it . . . Or even if we find Thurgood's crawler. We'll still be in trouble, but it may distract them a bit."

They argued about it. Marty felt he could not advance what weighed heaviest with him: the increasing longing to be back inside the Bubble, surrounded by the things and people he knew, taking the cabin to school, doing homework even . . . He realized Steve did not share this feeling. As the argument continued, he realized something else— that the people who had shaken their heads over him as obstinate and self-willed had not been all that far off the mark. Since they had palled up, Steve had seemed easygoing, willing to let Marty have the lead in things. There had been the balloons, but that was something Marty had accepted right away. Marty himself had suggested going to First Station, but that too was in line with what Steve wanted. This was the first time they had clashed sharply, and Marty found himself beaten back, bit by bit, by Steve's implacable determination. In the end, Steve had him maneuvered into a position in which he had either to agree to the new scheme or seem a coward, scared of having offended the authorities and afraid to do anything that would offend them further. So, unwillingly, he agreed.

"We'll go up there and have a look. But not hang around, searching, if we don't find anything. O.K.?"

Steve nodded. "O.K."

He seemed satisfied with his victory, but looked as though he had never been in doubt of it. Marty resented that and showed it. Steve in return was amiable. They worked it out that the co-ordinate point referred to would take seven or eight hours to reach, and he suggested that they should both get a sleep in before setting out. He insisted on Marty taking the bunk while he bedded down on the floor of the cabin.

But it was some time before Marty got to sleep.

At first he was being furious with himself over his own weakness. Later he was thinking of home and feeling miserable.

Their route lay south of the pass, in higher and more difficult ground than that which they had previously encountered. The crawler needed careful handling and three or four times they went off course and had to backtrack. Driving was an exhausting business and they switched to one-hour shifts; even an hour was tiring. But they were making progress: the red line traced on the map by the navigator slowly lengthened, snaking its way up through the hills, toward the distant mountains. At last, Marty said: "We're on it, as near as can be. 217-092. See any flowers?"

It was a torn and savagely splintered land, jagged and angular, much harsher even than the usual moonscape. Steve had had the grip-spikes out continuously for the past half hour and even so the crawler tended to slip and stagger. He halted now, and said: "That could be the cleft he went through just before he saw it, over there on the left. There's a bank of rock beyond with breaks in it. I'm going to try it anyway."

The fissures of which Thurgood had written were not only too narrow to get the crawler through but were also some feet above the floor of the little valley. Steve stopped the crawler again alongside one of them, and they stared out. The break looked across to a wall of rock, a hundred yards or so beyond. There was no sign of movement, no sign of anything but bare stone. Steve said: "I'm getting out to have a look."

Marty did not suggest accompanying him; it was routine that one person remained inside the crawler except in an emergency. He watched him go through the lock and then clamber awkwardly up inside the fissure so that he could see what lay on the other side. He stayed there some minutes. When he got back, Marty said: "Well?"

Steve shook his head. "Nothing. There's what looks like a small crater on the other side with a long drop beneath it. Nothing remarkable."

"So he must have been mistaken. Or mad. More probably mad since he took it so seriously. Do we go back now?"

Steve said: "What I think might be an idea is to

work around and see if we can get up *on* to the other side. There's a ledge which looks broad enough. We could see much better from there."

"See what? You've seen enough to know there couldn't be a giant flower here, or anything like a flower. What's the point in going on?"

"I think he must have been wrong," Steve said. "There's nothing but rock. But now we've come so far . . . I think we could try to spot his crawler. This is the place he was heading for."

"But once he got here," Marty argued, "and found he had drawn a blank, he may have traveled on. Perhaps by that time he was chasing giant butterflies."

"I don't think so. I think he would have hung around."

"In any case, the patrols from First Station that made the search for him will have come here. Mike Pozzi knew where it was. They must have worked that out."

Steve got back into the driving seat. "I'd like to have a look, all the same."

He spoke with the same inflexible determination. Short of fighting him over it, he was not going to be stopped. And quite apart from the fact that, as Marty had learned during their few wrestling bouts in the gymnasium at the Recreation Center, Steve was a lot stronger than he was, one did not start fights inside a crawler: the risks were too great. All he could do was bear with the situation and hope that Steve would soon get as bored with the business as he was already.

The going became even worse. Steve drove a tortuous course through the rocks, with the crawler at times balanced at precarious angles. Gradually, though, he worked his way past or around the various obstacles, and they reached the ledge he had spoken of. They were much higher than they had been. Below and in front of them was what Steve had thought was a crater, but from here one could see that it was more like a cone-shaped depression in the rock, no more than thirty feet across. Below it, the rock face fell into a gulf whose bottom could not be seen. Across lay the other face, broken by the fissures through one of which Steve had climbed.

Marty said: "I still don't see anything."

"You'll have to do the looking. This ledge . . ." Steve was concentrating on the controls. "It's narrower than I thought." The crawler's left-hand tracks dropped and they were traveling at an angle to the horizontal again. "Tricky."

"Want me to take a turn?"

"Not right now. You could make some coffee, but I would wait till we get level again. Keep your eyes skinned."

The ledge continued to narrow and continued to cant over to one side. Steve was proceeding very slowly, letting each spike bite home in turn. They were safe enough, but Marty found he was not enjoying the glimpses he had of the ravine on their left. It was possible that Thurgood had fallen down there—the early crawlers had been much less stable than modern ones were.

The ledge turned a corner ahead of them and from there was presumably directly above the cone-shaped depression. If it were any more narrow or oblique, Steve would have to reverse. They inched around, and could see what lay ahead. Steve gave a grunt of satisfaction.

"That's better."

The ledge broadened in front, extending into a shelf at least twenty-five feet across. That part was in shadow, but farther on there was a broad sunlit pass leading downward. Steve said: "We can move a bit faster now."

The engine whined on a higher note as he increased speed, retracting the grip-spikes at the same time. They rolled forward, moving into shadow. Marty said: "I think I'll see about that coffee."

"That's a brilliant idea. I was just . . ."

Steve wrenched violently at the wheel as, without warning, the crawler slid sideways. With one arm he slammed the grip-spike lever, to engage them again. But the crawler was out of control, loose stones screeching and whining under her tracks. A small patch of scree, Marty thought, masked by the shadow of the overhang above. It was the last logical thought he had before the crawler tipped over, falling free into space, and everything dissolved into fear and the certainty of death.

6

A Storm of Leaves

MARTY REMEMBERED CLOSING HIS EYES tightly as the crawler skidded and fell. He had no recollection of opening them again, but he realized he could see light. There had been the smack of impact which had thrown him hard against the bunk curtain. But a dragging, braking impact, followed by a second: sharp and final but not the annihilating crash which he had expected— which had seemed inevitable.

Not only light but color. It shimmered softly through the spectrum—reds and golds, greens and blues. A dream? He closed his eyes and opened them again. The colors were still there, and outside. He was seeing them through the observation dome of the crawler. And yet impossible. He looked for Steve and saw him slumped against the wall. He went to him, having to climb up because the crawler was at an angle, its nose pointing down. He said: "Steve . . ." and touched his hand. It seemed warm but there was no response.

Things were moving, high in the rainbow air. He looked up and saw them, and it was more fantastic than the colors. They were like leaves, a storm of them, but leaves that floated upward. Leaves, he thought . . . floating? Was he dead, perhaps? Was this the afterworld—heaven?

Dazed, he went to the airlock. It crossed his mind that he ought to put a suit on. But a spacesuit—to walk through paradise? He buttoned the inner door, stepped inside, and released the outer. He had not operated the air pump, but there was no hiss of escaping air. Instead air billowed in against him, pleasantly warm. It felt thick, heavy, rich to the lungs and sweet to the nostrils. He jumped down and his feet sank into a springy softness.

His eyes were growing accustomed to the light. It was altogether unlike anything he had known. Light on the Moon was full of harshness, hard blacks and whites with intermediate somber grays. This was gentle, flickering, continually changing, richly colored. He glanced down and saw that there was light at his feet, too. He stood on a carpet of something like moss and the carpet glowed green, mauve, dull amber. He walked and saw tiny stars of light splash from his treading feet. Splash? He bent down and touched with his fingers. Wetness clung to them. He had read of dew in meadows on Earth, small beads of brilliance hanging poised on spears of grass. Dew, on the barren Moon? If he were not dead he must be dreaming.

He could take in his surroundings better now. He was inside a cavern, some fifteen yards across and perhaps half that height. It was roughly circular but the floor sloped down. At the bottom it dipped quite sharply and there was what looked like the opening of a tunnel. The leaves . . . he raised his eyes, looking for them. A few still moved through the air but most seemed to have plastered themselves against the ceiling in a glowing patchwork. Light came from them, as it did from the moss. Phosphorescence—that was it.

By the far wall there was a moss-encrusted outcropping of rock. Farther up and in the middle of the cave he saw what at first looked like a giant snake. Giant indeed—more than a foot in thickness and lying in a huge elaborate coil. The body of it was black but the top swelled into a spheroid, creamy white, a couple of yards in diameter. Not a snake, he realized: the other end disappeared into the ground.

And yet that did not mean anything. In dreams nothing was fixed, everything capable of changing into something else. He watched to see if it would move. Nothing happened. Then he jumped as something lightly touched his cheek. He brushed at it frantically with his hand and saw a leaf go spinning away through the air, deepening from pink to crimson as it went. Two or three others were spiraling down toward him. He turned back to the crawler, jumped into the airlock and closed the door behind him.

He heard a noise as he came through the inner

door. From Steve—a small groan. Marty bent down and saw movement. He lifted Steve's head, and the eyes opened.

"You O.K.?" he asked.

"What happened?" Steve winced, momentarily closing his eyes again. "We hit that loose rock . . ."

"It's not a dream then." Marty felt almost disappointed. "People don't share dreams."

"Dreams? Where are we?" Steve struggled to his feet. "That light . . . is it real?"

"I don't know. It must be."

"What's that?"

Three of the leaves floated down and rested on top of the crawler. Two were pale lemon, the other a deep pulsating blue. After a moment the lemon-colored ones detached themselves and drifted up and away but the third remained.

"What is it?" Steve insisted.

Marty started to tell him as much as he knew. Steve interrupted to say: "You went outside? In a suit?"

"No." It seemed silly to say you did not need a spacesuit when you were dead. "I was a bit dazed."

"But you could *breathe*?"

"Yes. There's air, all right. It's different—scented, and it seems to make your lungs tingle. But you can breathe it. I was about five minutes out there."

"I don't believe it."

"Nor did I at first. We're in some sort of cave." It was beginning, in a weird way, to make sense; since they were obviously alive, it had to. "I suppose we're *inside* the Moon. We must have broken through the surface in that fall."

Steve shook his head and then put a hand up to it, grimacing.

"I must have landed on my skull." He paused. "I'm going out to have a look. How far did you explore?"

"Not far."

He was not going to say that a leaf had scared him.

"Come on then." Steve stopped by the airlock. "You're *sure* you went out. You didn't imagine it?"

Marty rubbed his fingers together; they were still wet.

"No, I didn't imagine it."

• • •

They stood in silence. The pattern of colors moved and spun along the walls and ceiling and floor of the cave. Steve spoke at last. He said: "Well, where?"

He had not spoken loudly but his voice had a slightly echoing quality. Marty said, keeping his own hushed: "What do you mean?"

"You said we'd broken through to the inside of the Moon. How? Where's the hole we made?"

It was a good point. All around and above them the colors ebbed and flowed in lambency. There did not appear to be a space a grip-spike could penetrate, let alone something as big as the crawler.

"Well, we're here," Marty said. "And I remember crashing. There were two impacts, the first a sort of dragging one. The second must have been when we dropped this last bit to the floor."

He remembered something else: the leaves which had been rushing through the air and which he had later seen plastered against the ceiling. He looked for them again and could not find them. That part of the cave's roof was no different from the rest, no leaf shapes showing in its kaleidoscope of shifting patterns.

He told Steve of this. Steve said: "Does that explain anything? I suppose it could." He stared around. "There has to be an explanation. Doesn't there? I mean, it can't be jabberwocky—it must have rules. We've only got to think them out."

Marty said: "I wonder . . ."

"What?"

"There's air in here, a bit denser than in the Bubble I would say. The cave has to be sealed or it would simply rush out into vacuum. The leaves floating up may have plugged the gap that was made when the crawler crashed through."

Steve objected: "It's not possible. How do you make a vacuum seal with *leaves*? And where are they now?"

"I don't know. But we're here, we're alive, and we must have got in some way."

Steve said: "It's crazy. Let's look around. We may find something."

They went up the sloping floor first. The moss

covered it completely. It was an inch or two deep and one could push one's fingers through to soil underneath. Reaching the wall they could see there was no dividing line—the moss climbed up without a break. Looking back they saw that the floor carried the same shimmering play of colors as walls and ceiling, except that where they had walked the imprints of their feet showed darker. But these gradually blended back into the colors and were lost. Steve pressed his hand against the wall at shoulder height.

"There can't be soil on a vertical surface. I thought not. So how . . . ? Wait a minute. Thin stalks running up. But what kind of plant could work that way?"

"What kind of leaves float upward?"

"Well, if there *were* a hole in the roof and air was blowing out I suppose the current would draw them up. Except that we still have the same nonsense of leaves sealing a gap between quite high air pressure and absolute vacuum. And where do the leaves come from? I don't see any trees around."

"There's that."

Marty pointed to the black snake-like coils, topped by the vast bud.

"No leaves, though."

Steve went over and Marty followed him. They ran their hands along it. The surface was very smooth and hard. The spheroid end was raised above the rest, some ten feet high. Steve jumped to try to touch it but failed.

"It moved a bit," Marty said.

"I didn't see. How?"

"A sort of swaying."

It was hard to describe. He felt uneasy. It had almost looked as though the movement had been a conscious one. But that was ridiculous. He said: "You probably shook it."

"No leaves anyway," Steve said. "And no sign of anywhere they could have been. There isn't a break on the whole of that surface. I'm going to take a closer look at that leaf which landed on the crawler."

But when they reached the crawler there was no sign of it. Steve stared around the cave.

"They have to come from somewhere. And go somewhere. What's that down there at the bottom?"

"It looks like a tunnel mouth."

Steve clicked his fingers. It was something which he did well and which Marty, despite hours of trying, could not do at all.

"That's it!" he said. "Of course. A tunnel. With an air current blowing through."

"Blowing which way?" Marty asked. "The leaves came and now they seem to have gone. And I can't feel a breeze, can you?"

The air was still and heavy and scented. Marty tried to think what the scent was like, but he had very little experience to go by. The Bubble was almost odorless, a place where the nose had very limited scope. This scent was not cloying but light, and subtly shifting like the colors.

The ground dipped sharply and they could see the tunnel. It went down at an angle of almost forty-five degrees. It was quite wide and had plenty of headroom. But for the slope it would have been easy to walk down.

"Maybe an intermittently varying air flow," Steve said.

"Caused by what?"

Steve stared into the tunnel. "I don't know. But the answer is down there. It has to be. There's nowhere else the leaves could have come from or gone to."

Uneasily Marty said: "I suppose you're right."

"So the obvious thing is to go and look."

"You don't know what's there."

"Leaves, I hope. And trees as well, I should think. Maybe Moon-birds nesting in them!"

"What I meant was, there could be a precipice or something. You won't get much purchase on the moss, on a slope like that. If you slipped . . ."

"I won't."

One could see a few yards into the tunnel, after which it twisted to the left. There was no way of knowing what lay past the bend.

Steve said: "No point in our both going down. You hang on up here."

Marty was not sure whether Steve had read the reluctance in his voice. He said angrily: "I'm going down if you are. I just thought . . ."

"I've got a better idea," Steve said. "Get a rope from the crawler. One goes down and one stays as anchor man. My idea, so I have the choice. Fair enough?"

It was obviously sensible. Marty went back to the crawler and fetched a coil of rope. Steve fastened it around his waist, pulling hard to check the knot.

"We're off, then. Take a strain."

He sat down and slid feet first into the tunnel. His body left a trail of phosphorescence on the moss. Marty stood with his feet apart and paid out rope. He saw Steve reach the bend and go around it. The rope came hard over against the wall on that side, cutting into the moss and disappearing beneath the shimmer. Marty hoped there wasn't a sharp edge under there.

Steve's voice came back, echoing: "All right from here."

"You're sure?"

"Yes. The tunnel levels. I can walk."

"I'll keep paying out."

"Right."

Marty stared about him as he let the rope through his hands. Against the pervasive glimmer the squat hulk of the crawler looked hard and yet unreal. Their refuge, he supposed. There was food for a few weeks. After that . . . He thought of being alone here, with the spheroid that shook on its vast black trunk, the leaves that came and went like ghosts or messengers . . .

How long since Steve had gone? Thirty seconds, a minute, five minutes? He had no idea. He looked at his finger-watch and saw that it was one-thirty. One-thirty a.m. that would be. Earth-time, Bubble-time. Time meant nothing in this glowing cave. Could it have been more than five minutes? The rope was no longer under tension but lying slack. Did that just mean that Steve had stopped going forward, or . . .

Steve's voice came up, muffled and very distant. So thin he could only just make out the words.

"Marty, come on down."

"Where are you?"

"It's all right. Come and see . . . It's fantastic."

He was still not keen on facing the tunnel but delaying would not help. He made the rope secure by knotting the end around one of the crawler tracks. Then he flung himself down the slope, sliding. The moss here was not actually wet, but damp and very springy. He got around the bend and found, as Steve had said, that the floor turned into an easy downward incline. The tunnel was very big; it would have taken the crawler with room to spare. He walked along toward another bend, to the right this time, and saw as he approached it that there was brighter light beyond. When he turned the corner he saw Steve sitting silhouetted against it. As Marty reached him, he said: "Look. It's unbelievable."

The tunnel emerged onto a ledge. They were near the top of a second cave, much bigger than the first, and there was an arch at the far end which provided a glimpse of a third. This cave was well over a hundred feet across, and they were perched at the top of a sixty- or seventy-degree slope, at least fifty feet above the floor. Walls and ceiling were covered with the moss but here it glowed with a steadier, whiter light. Down below . . .

Marty supposed you could call them trees, though they resembled no tree he had ever seen in books or on television. A tangle of trunks and stems and branches, ending in a riot of leaves of different shapes and colors. All brilliant—and all in motion! The trunks swayed, branches lifted and tossed, leaves shook as though in a gale. Yet up here the air was still. Perhaps not down there? He saw, though, that the movements were not uniform, not in any one direction. Two of the larger trees, as he watched, leaned in toward each other, their branches touching and mingling. And leaves from both detached themselves, lifted fluttering into the air, danced and spun in a wide fanning movement before settling down again.

He said: "The leaves . . . they went back onto the branches."

Steve said: "I know. Watch that!"

He pointed toward the far side of the cave, where there were no trees but a fuzzy greenish-purple stuff covered the ground. Part swelled up from the rest, became a prominence and then a ball that rose and hovered, bobbing, a dozen feet in the air. Others appeared and behaved in similar ways. After a few minutes it was possible to count five of them, dancing as the leaves had done, over and under and around each other, faster and faster until they seemed to blur into one.

"What are they?"

"I don't know. Look, they're changing."

The balls had ceased to spin and were sinking back toward the ground. One of them, though, did not. Instead it changed shape, becoming what looked like a pair of wings with no connecting body. The wings beat and it soared up until it was almost on a level with the ledge. Automatically Marty drew back, but it did not approach them. It flapped its way several times around the cave, then swooped down to the spot from which it had come. Purple-green ran into purple-green. There was a lump, a dissolving mound, finally the same flat surface there had been in the beginning.

They watched, fascinated but uncomprehending, for a long time. There was always something happening, some movement or eruption, brilliant and meaningless. Then Steve said he was hungry.

"You could try eating the moss," Marty suggested.

"I don't fancy it. It's probably poisonous, anyway. Let's go back to the crawler and get some food. We can come here again afterward."

He led the way up the tunnel, reeling in the rope.

When they reached the bottom of the slope, Marty said: "Better not take a strain on it unless you have to. I tied it to the crawler. We don't know how firmly anchored it is. We might pull it down on us."

"Good point. We should be able to jump it fairly easily."

He did not make it the first time, but Marty did. He stood at the top and gave Steve a hand to get up. The crawler was in the same place, but something else was different. There was no snake-like coil. The black trunk ran straight up from floor to ceiling, where the glowing moss closed tightly around it. So the spheroid must be outside.

Marty pointed to it. "Do you know what I think?"

Steve said it for him: "Thurgood's flower! It was in bud before. Now it's up there somewhere—probably opened out."

"But what for?" Marty asked. "To attract inter-planetary bees?"

"It's probably not a flower really. It could be absorbing sunlight. Plants live on solar energy. A chlorophyll conversion, or something similar. I wonder . . . could this all be part of one organism, one plant? And yet they're all separate—the leaves, the fuzz-balls, the bird-thing . . ."

Marty was looking past the black column at the moss-covered outcropping of rock he had noticed the first time he emerged from the crawler. He saw now how regular in shape it was, and that it did not actually join on to the wall. On the Moon's surface rocks sometimes had shapes that from a distance, in a certain light, could look artificial. It was probably no more than that, but he felt a new prickle of uneasiness. Thurgood's flower . . . which seventy years ago he had lost his life searching for.

He walked across the cave, and Steve followed him. The shape was more regular as they drew near, not less. A shape that beneath the blurring mask of moss was familiar. Standing by one corner, Marty reached down and pulled out a tuft. Light gleamed on metal, a section of crawler track.

They stared in silence for a few moments. Steve said at last: "So he found it, after all. He must have fallen through, the way we did."

"And then?"

Steve said slowly: "I suppose he's still inside.

We were very lucky not to break our necks."

Flesh did not decay in the lifeless vacuum of the surface, but there was air here and life. A skeleton, hunched over the controls—the only skeleton the Moon had ever known. Marty turned away, feeling sick. And frightened, because if Thurgood had not died in the crash then he had died later, more slowly and agonizingly, when his food gave out. They might be envying him yet. As they went back to their crawler, he said: "Do you think we ought to ration ourselves on supplies?"

Steve said gloomily: "I suppose so. Not that it's going to make much difference. It isn't as though anyone is likely to come looking for us. Even if the radio is still working, we can't transmit through rock."

They went into the crawler. The air felt musty and thin after the thick, sweet-smelling air of the cave. Marty kept his eyes away from the mossy wreck, but he was very much aware of it. He could not help wondering how long it would be before their own crawler looked like that.

7

A Face in a Dream

THEY HAD BROUGHT A STEEL SPIKE AND A hammer from the crawler, and Marty hammered the spike into the ledge to provide a holding point for the rope. When that was done and checked and the rope firmly secured, he watched Steve edge his way down the slope into the second cave. The trees swayed and waved as before, and he had a feeling that their branches were clutching upward toward the descending figure. He remembered the leaf that had brushed his cheek, and was afraid. Being plants they were mindless, of course, but that did not mean they could not be a menace.

There were plants on Earth that could trap and eat insects, and Earth plants did not have this fantastic ability to move.

But he had not opposed Steve's suggestion that they should explore the rest of the cave system. It was plainly something that had to be done. There was no hope of finding a way out from the top cave. Even if it were possible to locate the spot through which the crawler had crashed, they could not get at it. It was up in the roof of the cave, completely out of reach. They had to explore—the alternative was to sit and wait until their food supplies ran out, until they starved to death.

Steve was below treetop level. Marty watched as a nearby branch curled toward him, seemed to touch and stroke him, then drew back. Steve scrambled down the last few yards, and cast the rope free. He called up: "Everything O.K. Come on down."

Marty went down backward, bracing himself at each step, hanging onto the rope. He did not look around at the trees, but soon could hear the swishing of their branches through the heavy air. He told himself that since Steve had got down safely there was nothing to worry about. Except that the trees might be waiting to get both of them within reach before attacking them? That was silly, of course, because it implied thinking and trees could not think. All the same, his hair bristled.

He dropped the last few feet, and stood beside Steve. The branches tossed and twisted above their heads but did not come near them. The leaf touching him, the branch that stroked against Steve—they had probably been accidents. They must have been since plants could not see, either. But he still felt uneasy. Steve was examining the trunk of one of the trees. He said: "It's very smooth. Not bark, I think." He moved to unclip his belt-knife. "I wonder if it will cut easily."

Marty said: "No!" Steve looked at him. "I wouldn't do that, if I were you."

Steve looked up thoughtfully at the moving branches. "No, perhaps not. Let's head for that arch which seems to open into the next cave."

It was an eerie sensation walking under the threshing branches of the trees, and Marty was anxious to get to more open ground. When they reached it, though, he paused. This was the expanse of greenish-purple fuzz from which the flying balls and the flapping wings had emerged. He put out a tentative foot and found it different from the moss: softer, more deeply resilient. It even seemed to pulsate slightly, but that could have been an illusion. There was no sign of the surface swelling up, but he had the feeling it might happen at any moment. Steve led the way across, walking toward the arch, and Marty followed him.

They heard it first when they were almost across the fuzz, but so faint and distant that this, too, could have been something in the mind. He stopped. Steve said: "You hear that? It can't be."

They listened, straining their ears. More like the ghost of music than music itself, thin and far away. Marty said: "It's coming from somewhere ahead."

"I know."

It was more clearly audible as they went under the arch into the next cave. Something like an organ, Marty thought. And strangely familiar . . . Steve halted again. He said, in shocked disbelief: "I know that tune!"

Marty said: "I think I do, but I can't place it."

"It's one of those late twentieth-century things. A comic opera." He whistled a few bars in accompaniment. "But that's crazy, isn't it? It can't be real."

There had been a downward slope in both of the first two caves which was accentuated in this one. Most of the floor was covered with the fuzz, but strange-looking plants grew in places. There was a thicket of cactus-like things, spiked and eccentrically branched, in different shades of blue, and in another place a cluster of small bushes, almost perfectly spherical, gray streaked with splashes of brighter colors.

The rock wall on the right showed an uninterrupted glow of moss. On the left, though, and at the bottom there were openings. It was from one of these that the music must be coming. Several of the openings were above floor level, one of them halfway up to the roof. But they were not inaccessible. Looking closely, Marty saw that there were plants there as well. It was difficult to decide whether they were bushes or trees: what was important about them was that their branches, gnarled and twisted, rose up against the rock face, forming a natural ladder by which one could climb to the galleries.

Steve said: "I think the music is coming from the second one along."

He moved in that direction. Marty said: "Wait a minute."

"What for?"

"Those trees growing up the side of the cave toward the holes—they're almost like ladders."

"Well, yes. We can climb up quite easily."

"But they *only* grow under the holes, as though they're there just to act as stairways."

"True," Steve said. "I hadn't realized that."

"For us to climb up?"

"I see what you mean. There may be other things here as well as plants. Moon-men? Giant spiders? More likely to be humanoid, if they climb ladders."

"That doesn't explain why the ladder trees should be there and only there."

"The Moon-men could have planted them and trained them. Maybe they're great gardeners."

"And the music? Earth music?"

"They probably listen in on our radio."

Steve put one foot on the lowest crook of the tree. Marty said: "If there are Moon-men up there . . . they may not be friendly."

"That's also true," Steve said. "In which case we're unlucky. But I don't suppose we can go on dodging them indefinitely. We might as well find out the worst."

He climbed the tree and Marty followed him. The surface was rougher than that of the trees in the other cave, but seemed to be worn smooth in places—places, he realized, which were at roughly the right intervals to have been made by climbing feet. The music was louder. It changed, in mid-bar almost, to another tune which was vaguely familiar. He came up to the tunnel mouth and could hear it very plainly. Some kind of march.

This tunnel was much smaller. It was possible to walk in it but there was not a lot of room on either side, and at times it was necessary to stoop. The rock surface, as everywhere, was covered with the luminous moss. They walked through a tunnel of flickering light toward the sound of music. Then they were around a corner, and the new cave lay ahead.

It took Marty a moment or two to realize what was wrong. He had been expecting to see plants and trees similar to the ones they had already encountered, or perhaps even more exotic. There were trees and plants here, but they were wildly out of keeping with the others, or with anything he could have imagined. To start with, there was grass; lush green, calf high, extending almost to the tunnel mouth. He walked into it, bent down and held it in his hands. The only grass he had ever touched had been that in the park back in the Bubble, close-mown to a quarter of an inch. This was wild, riotous, luxuriant. He picked a blade and smelt a different scent, the smell of grass itself.

Steve had gone past him in the direction of the trees. He stood under one of them, and called: "Marty . . ."

The leaves were a darker green than the grass, the trunk gray-brown, rugose, branches twisted as though by the slow stresses of long years of growth and weather. Among the leaves there were pink and white blossoms, and round green fruit flushed with red.

Steve said in a dazed voice: "It's an apple tree."

Marty joined him. He said: "I know. One of the first things I remember in kindergarten was that apple in the picture book."

"But apple trees don't have flower and fruit on at the same time."

"Not on Earth. These are Moon-apples."

"It's an illusion," Steve said. "It has to be."

One of the branches hung down, with half a dozen fruit seeming to bow it low. Steve lifted one, weighing it in his open palm.

"It seems real enough." He plucked it off. "And smells good."

He lifted it to his mouth. Marty said: "Do you think you should?"

"Why not?"

"I was thinking of what you said about the moss: that even if one could eat it it would probably be poisonous. Isn't that true of these? We don't know anything about their chemical structure."

Steve turned the apple over in his hand. It was not quite round; flattened at the stem end, slightly pointed at the other. Apple shape, in fact. Marty could smell it, distinct and individual like the grass.

"It looks all right," he said.

Marty could feel his own half-abated hunger pangs stirring. He said, trying to convince himself as much as Steve: "It's taking a big chance."

Steve said: "What difference does it make? We've got provisions in the crawler for six weeks maybe, if we ration ourselves tightly. After that, we starve. We have to take a chance on it sometime."

"We might learn more during the month," Marty said. "Maybe . . ."

His words trailed off. He had been intending to say they could use the time in trying to escape, but even as he framed the proposition he saw how futile it was. They were trapped inside a mountain which in turn was surrounded by the lifeless vacuum of the Moon. There was no hope at all of getting the crawler out. There was almost as little prospect of finding a way out on foot, which in any case would mean using spacesuits. They could carry a couple of cylinders of air at a pinch and a little food concentrate. Somebody had once spent eight hours in a spacesuit and survived, but he had been in a hospital for weeks afterward. And in eight hours on foot you would be doing well to cover twenty-five miles. The range of the suit radios was well under a mile.

Steve said: "Well, here goes," and bit into the fruit.

"What's it like?" Marty asked.

"Sensational."

He went on eating. Marty picked one himself and bit into it. Juice spurted against his chin. At home he had eaten apple-flavor puddings, of the same mushy consistency as most food in the Bubble. That taste had done nothing to prepare him for this—the sweetness, tartness, indefinable something. And the texture, of juiciness combined with firmness.

He finished it and, after hesitating, dropped the core in the grass. From earliest childhood he had been trained in the lunar discipline of no-waste, no-mess, but here there was neither a recovery nor a garbage receptacle. He wondered what the organic cycle was in the caves. Were there bacteria to break things down so that they could be reabsorbed? He

shook his head. It was like worrying about a foot-
note in a book written entirely in gibberish.

Steve was eating his second apple. Marty was
about to do the same thing when he saw something
else. It was a little way down from the apple tree,
and not a tree so much as a large plant. The overlapping bases of big glossy leaves formed a false
trunk from which a head emerged; and the head in
turn carried perhaps a dozen clusters of long,
slightly curving yellow fruits.

He went to look, and Steve came after him.

"Apples," Steve said, "and now bananas. It gets
crazier and crazier, doesn't it? As though things had
been laid on for us, prepared in advance."

Marty stretched up and took two bananas off
one of the clusters. He threw one to Steve.

"Catch. Or do you want to wait and see how the
apples go down?"

He broke the skin and peeled it and bit off an
end. Here again the real thing was vastly different
from the artificial flavorings he was used to. Steve,
eating the other one, said: "You can almost live off
bananas, can't you? They have protein, don't they?

In that book I was trying to write I had one of my pirates marooned on a Pacific island and living on bananas and coconuts, and what fish he could get out of the lagoon. Do you think we could be living inside someone's book?" He looked around. "If so, he fills in a pretty solid background."

They moved on. They were in an orchard, but one made up of many and diverse trees. There were pears, the fruit a deep golden color, the skin seeming on the point of bursting with juice. They saw peaches, pomegranates and, scenting the air for a great distance, half a dozen trees with oranges nestling among dark green leaves. In an open patch pineapples grew side by side with strawberries, and farther on they found a thicket of raspberry canes. There were yet other trees with fruits they did not recognize at all. They ate as they went, until they were full.

Marty said: "I don't think I can manage any more."

"There's always tomorrow."

"Unless the Moon-men run us in for trespass and theft. I've been thinking—have you seen any insects?"

"No."

"Ought there not to be some?"

"Why?"

"Well, these are plants and they have flowers and fruit. I was thinking of pollination."

"Plants on Earth have to have insects because they're all fixed in the ground. This organism has moving parts: remember the leaves and the fuzz-balls."

"Not in this cave."

"I suppose they could come in here when they were wanted. The leaves moved from one cave to another."

"Do you think it is all part of one organism, using the flower for energy?"

"I don't know. It could be."

"And the Moon-men?"

"We still haven't found them."

"I've been thinking," Marty said. "If we could get news of this place back to our folks. We could all abandon the Bubble. People could live here."

"Yes," Steve said. "Bring everyone in. Blast a hole in the side of the mountain and put in an airlock so crawlers can go in and out. Smash another gap in the roof of the top cave for an observation ceiling. Build houses and laboratories and a school, not forgetting a Recreation Center. And string wires all over the place, so no one has to walk more than five yards. I should think the plants and trees are going to look a bit sick by the time you've done a tenth of all that."

"I suppose so," Marty said. "And we can't get news out anyway. That music's a lot nearer. It must be coming from just past the next bunch of trees."

They walked through and stared up at it in silence. This also was a tree, Marty supposed—at least it grew out of the ground and had what could possibly be described as branches. But the branches were in the shapes of long straight pipes in one place, taut wire-like tendrils in another. Still other branches plucked at the tendrils or sawed across them. The music changed into a syrupy waltz, which involved quite a lot of activity in that direction.

"An orchestra-tree," Steve said. "And one that plays itself. I wouldn't say I admire its taste all that much, but it's quite an achievement for a tree."

"We are dreaming," Marty said. "We must be. But whose dream is it? Yours or mine—or someone else's?"

"The one who's writing the book, maybe." Steve felt with thumb and forefinger for a strand of hair at his temples, grimaced, and tugged a hair out. "I'm not dreaming."

If you looked carefully, you could see that there were holes in the pipe-like branches, through which air was presumably sucked or blown. What would be the mechanism of that, Marty wondered? It would be interesting to climb the tree and examine it. He looked again and decided he was not sufficiently interested to try. The thought of going up among those blowing pipes and sawing strings was more than a little scarifying.

He turned away and, as he did so, had a glimpse of something farther on. It was just a blue flatness, seen through a gap between fruit trees. He went that way and called to Steve. They stood looking at it together. The trees ended, giving way to a lawn, the grass short and velvety green. And the lawn ran down to the still, blue, gleaming waters of a lake.

Steve said at last: "There had to be a reservoir of some kind. Plants can't grow without water. How did it get here in the first place, though?"

How did any of it get here, Marty thought? There were too many questions—or the same question repeated from a hundred different angles—and there had to be answers somewhere. He went across the lawn to the water's edge. At that point the grass ended and the familiar moss took over again, running out under the lake and lighting it from below. He looked automatically for fish but could see nothing. The waters were clear and empty. He dipped his fingers in. The temperature was only a degree or two less than that of the air. One could swim in it comfortably. He looked along the lake. It occupied the full width of the cave, under the arching moss-covered roof. At the end . . . he could not be sure but it looked as though cave and lake twisted away to the right.

He said: "I wonder how far these caves go. For miles, maybe."

"Yes." Steve's voice was abstracted. Marty turned from the water and saw that he was looking up at the roof of the cave. He said in a slightly puzzled voice: "Marty . . ."

"Yes?"

"Do you notice anything about the light?"

"From the moss? I don't think . . . Wait a minute. Is it dimmer than it was?"

It was happening very gradually. At first he could not be sure whether the light really was a shade less bright, or whether he had been influenced by Steve's question. But soon the darkening was unmistakable. The glow was fading from the moss-covered ceiling and walls, and the blue of the lake was deeper as its radiance drained away. The fading became more and more rapid.

Shaken, Marty said: "What do you think this is?"

It was very dark, and even as he spoke blackness came down on them. Steve said: "I don't know. Could be temporary, I suppose. I hope so."

They waited, but there was no change in the darkness. After the first surprise, they had taken for granted the fact of being able to see their way, of being surrounded by light and color. It was frightening to be forced to realize again where they were:

trapped in the bowels of this alien world. If they had stayed in the first cave they would at least have had the crawler, with lighting as long as the batteries held out. They had not even brought flashlights with them. They had not seemed necessary, but it had been careless not to take the precaution. It would be a difficult and perilous job to find their way back there now.

Steve beside him said: "I'm going to lie down. Might as well be comfortable while we wait for the lights to go up again."

It was reassuring to hear his voice. Two were better than one. Marty said: "How long do you think?"

"There's no knowing, is there? An hour, perhaps. Or a day. Or a century."

That last thought was chilling. Marty argued: "It can't be too long a time. The trees must have had regular days."

"That would be true on Earth, but we don't know about Moon-trees. We don't even know if they are still there. The orchestra-tree has stopped."

The music had faded with the light. There was

only silence and blackness and their own small echoing voices. What if the caves had days a century long, and they had chanced on them as evening was merging into night? It did not seem likely, but probability had gone by the board from the moment of finding themselves in the first cave.

They talked together, in companionship against the darkness, discussing what they had found in the caves and trying yet again to find a meaning in them. They did not progress very far, over and over coming around to the same contradictions and bafflement. Gradually conversation lapsed, the gaps between talk lengthening. After one such gap, Marty said: "If there are Moon-men, how do they manage in the darkness? And there must be some sort of inhabitants. It doesn't make sense otherwise. Anyway, I'm sure those were footmarks on the ladder trees."

There was no answer from Steve. After a pause, he said: "Don't you agree? I mean, the orchard has to be *for* people. Hasn't it?"

Steve still did not reply. His breathing was deep and even. Marty realized he had fallen asleep. He lay back, stretching himself on the grass. It was softer than the lawn back in the Bubble. He tried to answer his own question about the Moon-men. How *did* they manage in the dark? But perhaps they were nocturnal, and could see, like cats. In which case . . .

He sat bolt upright, and then relaxed. That was nonsense: there were no cat-men advancing on them through the blackness. One would hear them coming. Except that another thing he knew about cats, even though he had never seen one, was that they trod lightly, noiselessly stalking their prey. He started to lean over, to shake Steve and wake him, and checked himself. It would be stupid to do that. His imaginings were stupid, anyway.

All the same, his nerve endings quivered. He tried lying down, but could not rest. He found himself cramped, whatever position he adopted. It was not the fault of the ground, he knew—Steve was sleeping peacefully—but of his own tension. He checked his finger-watch again and again as the slow minutes dragged by. The darkness had lasted nearly two hours. It seemed a lot longer.

. . .

At last he slept, and had a nightmarish dream in which the caves and the Bubble were all mixed up, and Mr. Sherrin was lecturing him for having sent up a mass of balloons which turned into leaves and suddenly came down, whirling around their ears. He drifted back to consciousness as he was trying to tell Mr. Sherrin that it was all right—they would go away again—and saw that the light had returned: the moss was glowing all around as it had done before. Sleep and the dream still pressed on him and confused him, but he realized that someone was standing near, a face looking down.

"Steve!" he said. "What do you think . . . ?"

That was when he came properly awake, and sat up in shock and fear. For the face was not Steve's, but that of a bearded stranger.

8

The Fruit of the Lotus

THE BEARD WAS LONG AND BLOND, ungroomed. Like the hair which fell to shoulder level it was slightly curly. Where it was not bearded or moustached, the face was white, pallid in the moss's glow. Their own skins showed pale in this light, but the stranger's was paler. Emerging from his first instinctive fear, Marty tried to read expression in the face looking down into his. It was difficult to make anything of it. The look was neither friendly nor hostile, but detached.

Marty scrambled to his feet. He felt a little less

vulnerable standing up. He said to the man: "Who are you? How did you get here?"

He realized as he spoke that if this were an inhabitant of the Moon he could scarcely be expected to understand English. On the other hand there was the orchestra-tree which was playing again, just switching from a familiar march to something which sounded like Johann Strauss. The man did not reply and they stared at each other in silence, wary on Marty's part, enigmatic on the man's. He was wearing shorts made out of what looked like large leaves sewn together; his body also was very white, lacking pigmentation.

Steve was still asleep. Marty reached down and shook him, and he opened his eyes.

"What . . . ?" He looked past Marty at the man, and jumped into life. He said sharply: "Who's that?"

"I don't know," Marty said. "I asked him but he didn't answer. He probably didn't understand."

"My name . . ." The stranger had a deep voice which spoke slowly and trailed off. "It's so long . . ."

Steve said: "I think . . . But it can't be, can it?"

He shook his head, bewildered. "It is, though." He stared at the man. "You're Andrew Thurgood. Aren't you?"

The man nodded, a small inclination of his head. Marty saw it too, now. Take away the beard and moustache and the face was familiar from that picture gallery of lunar pioneers, the men of First Station. Andrew Thurgood—the man who had not returned, whose crawler they had found in the first cave, scarcely recognizable beneath its covering of moss. How long was it? Seventy years. But this was quite a young man, not someone who, even if he had managed to survive, would have been a century old. Yet it was Thurgood.

They looked at him in awe, and Marty felt his fear returning. A ghost, maybe? The ghost of the man who had come here before them, and died here, warning them of what their own fate must be. But a ghost with a beard, wearing shorts made out of leaves? The absurdity of the notion was reassuring.

There had been a silence which Steve broke, asking: "Is there anyone here in the caves with you?"

Thurgood shook his head. Steve persisted: "I don't just mean men. Aliens, maybe. Moon-men?"

"Only the Plant."

"The Plant? What's that?"

Thurgood shrugged. It was the most human gesture he had made so far, an expression of inadequacy. Steve waved his arm toward the cave and the things growing in it.

"Are you saying all these are parts of a single plant, even though they're so different? But how can they be?"

Thurgood was silent. Steve pointed to the orchestra-tree. "That, as well?"

Thurgood spoke again. "Yes." He paused. "I'm sorry if I'm slow. At one time I used to talk a lot. To myself, you understand. Lately I haven't done that."

Apprehension was wearing off a little. Not a ghost but a man stumbling over his speech, someone who could be at a loss for words.

Steve asked: "Do you know what year this is?"

Thurgood shook his head.

"It's 2068," Steve said. He looked at Thurgood,

who said nothing. "Did you have any idea how long you had been here?"

"No. I knew it was a long time."

Marty asked: "Have you been in some sort of sleep? Suspended animation—like Rip van Winkle?"

"Not that I know of. I sleep when it's dark, wake when the light comes back."

Steve said: "You're over a hundred years old. But you're no different from the pictures of you, except for the beard."

Thurgood pulled his beard with his hand. "It got to this length and then it stayed. Are you from First Station?"

"No, the Bubble. First Station was abandoned more than fifty years ago. But why haven't you aged at all?"

Thurgood shrugged. "Time doesn't exist here."

"But things do grow! Those trees, for instance. There's an apple tree that must be twenty years old."

"Well, they're all part of the Plant, as I say. They grow from the Plant, and eventually the Plant will reabsorb them. There's no time, only change."

"But you haven't changed."

Thurgood wrinkled his brow. "I used to wonder about that. I suppose the Plant keeps me young. Over a hundred, you say? Maybe it's the fruit in the orchard. Don't I remember something about an apple of eternal life? Could be this is where it grew."

Marty asked: "How did those trees get here? You didn't have seeds with you, surely?"

"I've told you. The Plant makes them."

"But why? Just for your benefit?"

"Yes. There's no one else. Or wasn't till you came."

"But why?"

"Well, human beings have to be nourished. Human bodies need fueling. We can't live on sunlight the way the Plant does."

"They're copies of Earth fruit, though," Steve said. "Apples, pears, peaches."

"Those," Thurgood said, "and others."

"But how can the Plant produce things it doesn't . . ." Marty stopped, shaken. "Are you saying that you asked the Plant for them, and it grew them? That the Plant is an intelligent being?"

"Of course it is. I thought you'd realized that."

He looked surprised at the question. Of course, Marty realized, he had had longer to get used to the idea.

He said: "And it evolved here, on the Moon? But how? The Moon never was capable of sustaining life, was it? Or are the scientists wrong about that?"

"No, not on the Moon."

"But not on Earth, surely?"

"The Earth was too hot for life when the Plant came here."

"Too hot! But there has been life on Earth for millions of years—hundreds of millions. Are you saying this Plant thing has been in these caves as long as that?"

Thurgood said: "Time means nothing to the Plant."

Steve asked: "Where *did* it come from?"

From another, much older galaxy, he told them, traveling in spore form, blown by the wind of solar radiation. It had been a journey that lasted count-less aeons, of a seed in search of the landing place where it could lodge and grow and flourish. Certain conditions had to be present—certain chemicals and minerals and a particular level of solar energy. Many planets, possibly thousands, were found and rejected by the seed's instinctive intelligence. At last it found what it was looking for on the smaller of the twin planets circling third in orbit around this sun. The larger planet was too hot but the smaller, more rapidly cooling, was habitable.

"Habitable?" Marty asked. "You mean there was air and water?"

"Not in that form. But there was free oxygen, hydrogen, carbon dioxide."

"And the Plant could turn them into air and water, without machines?"

"Plants on earth convert sunlight into energy. It's no stranger than that. Only more powerful and purposeful."

"The Flower——" Steve said. "Does that do something similar?"

There had been, Thurgood explained, an initial period of absorption and growth. After that the Plant was fully mature and needed only solar radiation to maintain itself. This was achieved through the Flower, which uncoiled at intervals, thrust upward, and drank in the hot rays of the sun. It was a process something like photosynthesis but more efficient.

"And there's a break in the rock cover just there?" Steve asked. "I suppose there has to be, to enable the Flower to go in and out. So you saw the Flower and came looking for it and your crawler fell through, and now we've done the same."

"Why does the Plant need the protection of rock, anyway?" Marty asked. "If it can seal itself against vacuum, why bother to hide in caves?"

There were several reasons, Thurgood said. Partly protection against meteorites, partly concealment. The Plant thought in terms not of years but of millennia. And in addition there would be an energy imbalance in maintaining a thermal equilibrium without the insulation afforded by the natural rock. The Flower might not be able to replace the energy lost that way.

"The floating leaves I saw just after we crashed," Marty said, "plastering themselves against the roof of the cave—I suppose they were mending the seal which our crawler broke?"

Thurgood nodded. "There are three or four places where faults existed when the Plant came here, or where they have developed since. The sealing is automatic, like blood clotting in mammals."

"It must have lost some air, though."

"A little, but it is unimportant. The concentration is richer than is strictly needed."

"That's something else," Steve said. "There's oxygen here—it's a breathable atmosphere. But oxygen's a waste product as far as plants are concerned. They breathe carbon dioxide, don't they?"

Marty said: "They synthesize sugars out of carbon dioxide and water, but carbon dioxide is soluble in water." He looked at the lake. "There could be plenty there."

"I still don't see what it does with the oxygen," Steve said. "If it is a waste product, then it would build up all the time. And this is supposed to have gone on for millions of years."

Thurgood said: "The Plant evolved into a state of perfect harmony and balance. The thinking part is different from the rest, and it consumes the oxygen."

"What about your coming here," Marty asked, "and then us? Doesn't that interfere with the perfect balance?"

"A little, but the Plant can cope with it."

"Look," Steve demanded, "how do you know all this? All the stuff about the way the Plant came here, and how it's organized. Are you telling us you can talk to it?"

"Yes. Of course."

"Then what do you do? Stand in front of the banana plant and ask questions, and one of the bananas opens up and talks back?"

"You will find out," Thurgood said, "in due course."

"You mean it will talk to us?"

"If it wishes."

"It knows we're here?"

"Except during meditation, the Plant is aware of everything that happens in every part of the caves."

"Meditation?"

"That's when the light goes. The Plant withdraws into its inner self and meditates."

"Meditates on what?" Steve asked.

"On itself."

"That sounds pretty dull."

"You don't understand yet," Thurgood said. "You couldn't be expected to. The wisdom of the Plant is something human beings can't ever grasp properly." He spoke with patience but also with conviction. "It's a different kind of thinking from ours. Men are always thinking in terms of doing things—building bridges and machines, exploring the universe. The Plant is sufficient in itself. It doesn't need to make anything or go anywhere."

"I still think it sounds dull," Steve said.

Thurgood looked as though he might be going to reply, but did not. After a moment, he said: "Don't know about you, but I'm hungry. Feel like a little breakfast?"

They walked up toward the fruit trees. Marty said: "You live on these, and nothing else?"

"You don't need anything else," Thurgood said.

"I don't see how it can be a balanced diet—just fruit."

"The Plant sees to that. I'm alive and well, aren't I?"

He certainly looked fit enough. Pale-skinned, though that might be partly an effect of the peculiar light from the moss, but otherwise he seemed perfectly healthy. And young, instead of being a tottering centenarian. He stood in front of the cluster of orange trees, examining them. He said to the boys: "Signs of heavier fruiting already. That's to make allowance for you two being here. They don't take as long to grow as fruit does back on Earth—no more than a few hours from flower to ready for eating. Catch."

He threw a couple of oranges to them. They peeled and ate them, walking through the orchard, and picked other fruits. Thurgood had been right in saying they grew quickly: the belt of raspberry canes, which he remembered denuding on their first visit, was not only starred with white flowers but heavy with fruit, most of it ripely red. And new canes were springing from the ground; he almost thought he could see them grow.

The boys lost touch with Thurgood at some point. He was still missing when, their stomachs full, they wandered back to the lawn grass that stretched down to the lake. Steve called him: "Mr. Thurgood! Mr. Thurgood . . ."

There was no reply. Marty said: "He could be anywhere. Anywhere in the caves, that is."

He flopped on the grass, and Steve followed suit. Steve said: "Funny he didn't say where he was going, though—or that he was going."

"A lot of things are funny," Marty said. "He asked if we were from First Station, and you said no, we were from the Bubble. You would think he would have been a bit curious about that, that he would have wanted to know what things were like outside. But he didn't ask a single question. He left all the questioning to us."

"I suppose when you are a hundred years old you could lose interest in things."

"But he's not a hundred years old—not in that sense, anyway. He said it: time doesn't mean anything here. He hasn't changed from the day he came in except to grow a beard. He's the same man he was, so why isn't he curious about all the things that have happened since then? Think of the things he doesn't know about: airsphering, brain transplants, the South American War . . ."

Steve said: "He probably needs to get used to not being by himself. It's a long time to be a Robinson Crusoe."

The orchestra-tree was playing a selection of airs from what was probably a forgotten musical comedy: deservedly forgotten, as Steve commented. He asked: "Do you think we could get a different brand of music if we asked the Plant nicely? But we don't know where you put the requests in, do we? I suppose we could do a little exploring and see if we can find out."

They went back through the cave and the tunnel, and down the ladder tree. Up there in the top cave their crawler still presumably lay by the stem of the Flower. Marty wondered if the moss had yet begun to grow, ever so slightly, over the crawler's tracks. Steve was leading the way toward another ladder tree, another opening in the cave wall, and Marty followed him.

The tunnel here was steep and narrow, forcing them to crawl at times. They came out into a cave smaller than any they had seen so far. Moss covered the walls, but its light was dimmer and grayer than in other places. In this dusk they discerned tall gray mushroom-like shapes which at first sight seemed perfectly still. Watching, though, it was possible to detect movement, a slow, slow oscillation of the mushroom caps on the long, gently yielding stems. Nothing else happened. They stared for minutes, and then withdrew.

In the second cave they tried there was another orchestra-tree. It was much larger than the one by the lake and much louder, but the music—if it was music—was entirely different. It struck at the ears, raucous, tuneless, full of discords and flat notes. And to it a weird company of plant-things danced an incomprehensible jig—some rooted, some flying free. They were of all colors, and the colors were as harsh to the eyes as the sounds to the ears, somehow sharper and more wrenching than the colors of the familiar spectrum. Marty wanted to turn away at once, but Steve insisted on staying, trying to make sense of it.

"It's a kind of ballet," he said. "At least, that's the nearest one can get to it."

"Not likely to hit the Top Ten on Network TV."

Steve said: "You can almost get something at times. Just then, for instance." He made a face. "And right away it goes sour."

"It never went sweet as far as I was concerned," Marty said. His eyes and head were beginning to ache from the din and the kaleidoscopic dazzle. "I think I'll leave you to sort it out."

Steve shook his head. "I don't really think I want to."

They found a cave thickly covered with something that was vaguely like grass, except that it was dark red and looked as though it were at least nine feet deep. A curious rippling movement ran through it from time to time, as though things were moving down below the surface. The boys ventured no farther than the tunnel mouth. There was an entrance to yet another cave on the far side, but the thought of wading through the red rippling grass stuff to reach it was not a tempting one.

One cave was, except for the glowing moss, entirely empty. They stood in the center and looked around at the shimmering blankness.

"Did the Plant run out of ideas," Marty asked, "or is this one lying fallow?"

"I don't know," Steve said. "We could ask Mr. Thurgood. If we find him again. You could lose each other for days in this warren."

Marty cupped his hands around his mouth and hallooed. The sound echoed strangely in the silence, and he stopped quickly. Somewhere not far away in the cave system the two orchestra-trees were very likely still giving out their different kinds of music, but here there was a hushed stillness. The rock would provide perfect insulation, of course. All these small separate worlds and yet each, if Thurgood were to be believed, sustained and controlled and watched over by the Plant. Presumably it could see them now, hear their voices. What would it make of these two intruders in its domains—how would it react to them? Marty shivered, and then remembered they were not the first. Thurgood had been here for seventy years, not only unharmed but cherished by the Plant. Only a few hours ago it had seemed that they must resign themselves to dying of starvation. That fear at least was ended.

They went on and came to a cave studded with clumps of snake-like things that rose, writing, out of the moss. The boys threaded their way between the clumps, instinctively giving them a wide berth. There was nothing to fear in the caves, Thurgood had assured them, but there was plenty to make one uneasy by its weirdness. A thought came to Marty, and he said: "If the darkness came again while we were here . . . I wouldn't fancy sleeping among this lot. Nor of finding a way back through it."

"No," Steve said. "Me neither. We could go back to the lake cave. I've done enough exploring for today."

Thurgood was there, lying on the grass by the lake. Marty said something about losing him, and he smiled but did not volunteer anything about where he had been. The boys talked about their own explorations, and he listened incuriously. They asked him questions about the various caves they had found, and the things in them, to which he gave vague, unhelpful answers. Yes, he thought the empty cave had not always been empty; in fact he could remember a kind of spinning merry-go-round in it at one time. And no, he did not think there was anything actually moving under the red grass—just the grass itself in motion. All these were parts of the mysteries of the Plant. One could not expect to understand them.

Later they went back up the slope to the orchard. Thurgood showed them things they had not previously discovered, or which they had not risked eating. There were reddish fungi, growing in abundance near one wall, which had a pleasant meaty taste, and round yellow turnip-like roots which tasted of cheese. These were probably protein sources, Marty thought. He also showed them the drinking-fountain tree. It resembled a palm and one parted the outer leaves to reveal, in the center, a pool of clear liquid in which one could cup one's hands and drink. The liquid was almost tasteless but not quite; there was a hint of lemon. They drank deeply and Marty noticed that more liquid was forming on the inside of the sword-like leaves, trickling down to augment the pool.

They drifted back in the direction of the lake. Steve asked if it were possible to swim in it.

Thurgood said: "Yes. I used to at one time. I can't remember how long since. The Plant made me a swimming place. There was a tree with branches I used to dive from . . ."

"Could it do that again," Steve said, "if you asked it?"

There was no reply. Steve repeated his question. Marty looked and saw that Thurgood was moving slowly, falling behind them. He looked as though there were a weight on his shoulders. Marty noticed something else: the light of the moss was starting to dim again. Thurgood yawned and, in a collapsing movement, dropped to lie in the long grass.

Steve said: "Mr. Thurgood . . ."

They went back and stood over him. Marty said: "He's asleep."

Light drained, slowly at first and then more and more rapidly, from the cave. In the end there was blackness. It was less frightening than the first time because they knew what was happening and that it was only temporary. They sat side by side in the dark, and Marty said: "It would be a good idea to get flashlights down from the crawler."

"It hardly seems worth it. We might as well get into the habit of sleeping during the dark times. He does."

Marty said: "He went out like a light, didn't he? *With* the light. Except that he looked as though he were beginning to go off even before the light started dimming."

Steve said: "I suppose you become conditioned after seventy years. And more sensitive to the light as well. He's probably aware of it dimming before we are."

It still seemed odd to Marty. Steve, though, switched back to the subject he had been on earlier: the possibility of swimming in the lake. Was it really possible that the Plant could make a special swimming place, and grow a tree one could dive from? It seemed incredible, but in view of everything else . . .

They talked about this and the caves for some time before sleep claimed them. Once again it was Steve who fell asleep first.

9

The Worshiper

MARTY WAS AWAKENED BY A HAND THAT shook his shoulder. He mumbled: "What's the matter, Steve?" and then, coming awake, saw that Thurgood was the shaker. It was light again. Steve was standing just beyond Thurgood, who now said: "The Plant wants to see you."

"How did it send the message," Marty asked, "—by flying-leaf mail?"

Thurgood did not bother to reply. He started down toward the lake and the boys, after an exchange of shrugs, followed him.

It floated just touching the grassy bank that

formed the shore of the lake. It was about six feet square, and seemed to consist of overlapping flat green pads. They stood and looked at it. Thurgood said: "Climb aboard."

His voice was not exactly impatient but not quite so unconcerned and lackadaisical as usual. Marty said: "Is it a raft? It won't bear us, surely."

"It will bear you," Thurgood said.

He put his own foot out and depressed the near edge, which was raised several inches above the surface of the water. It dipped a little, but not much. Steve stepped out on it and his weight scarcely seemed to depress it at all. Marty followed.

He said: "I wonder what gives it buoyancy?" He bent down and probed between the surface leaves. "I think this lower part has pods, like seaweed."

"We're moving," Steve said. "But how?"

Marty looked and saw the shore receding from them. Thurgood stood watching them. Marty called: "Aren't you coming?"

Thurgood shook his head without answering. The gap between plant-raft and shore was widening fairly rapidly. Old fears came back. A raft that moved of its own volition, taking them somewhere but they did not know where . . . there was a feeling of helplessness, of being in the power of something utterly strange.

Steve said: "A current, do you think?" He knelt and put a hand in the water. "It seems absolutely still."

They tried to work out the mechanism of the raft's motion but got nowhere. It was at least comforting to talk in objective terms, as a means of forgetting the strangeness of the journey. The lawn and the orchard fell farther behind, and it was possible to see that the cave and the lake did bend, that each extended to the right. Marty said suddenly: "We don't have to do any of this. Just because Thurgood told us."

"It's a bit late now to think about refusing."

"We could dive off," Marty argued, "and swim back. The water's not cold and Thurgood swims in the lake, or used to."

Steve said doubtfully: "I suppose we could. But do you think it's wise to antagonize the Plant, whatever it is?"

It was a point which was valid but which Marty did not enjoy contemplating. They were in its grasp, subject to whatever incalculable whims it might have. There might be some way of fighting it, of killing it even and finding a way out, but until they knew more about its nature and its capabilities, defiance would be both rash and foolish.

Steve said: "The light's different over there. Brighter. Do you see?"

It was reflected on the water and the cave wall from a source still hidden by the bend. As the raft took them around, it increased in strength. They cleared the last part of the curve, and saw it: a column of golden light that hung down from the cave roof. No, that was wrong. It did not descend, but rose. At the bottom there was an island, and the light came up from that, a honey-colored searchlight so bright that it almost seemed solid.

The boys were silent. Was it hot, Marty wondered? It looked as though it might be—a pillar of fire which could sear and scorch the flesh. Perhaps this was a trap and Thurgood had deliberately led them into it. Perhaps he was not even Thurgood at all, but a phantasm produced by the eerie, incalculable being which lived here. Their raft and they might drift on, to a fiery death—in the burning maw, maybe, of the ruler of the caves.

He wondered if he should not even now dive into the water and swim away, but even as he thought of this his fear left him. The column of light was still more dazzling as they approached it but no longer terrifying. He was puzzled by that. It was not because of a change in anything he could see. The difference was deep down in his mind, a sense of peace and assurance. If it were a furnace they were drifting toward, it would not hurt him. He was sure of it.

The island was clearly visible, less than thirty feet distant. Its shore scarcely rose above the water's level, but all around it was surrounded by huge fronds, of more than a man's height, which swayed in a gentle continuous motion. They were deep red in color, so deep as to be nearly black. The light which formed the column was contained by them, and here and there spilled through in spears of brightness.

The raft touched land and automatically, not thinking what they were doing, the boys stepped on shore.

The peace and assurance were still in Marty's mind, but there was something else as well: a deep sense of awe. It was the sort of feeling he had had at times in seeing the lunar dawn flare between the eastern mountain peaks; in looking at the full misty globe of Earth or at the scattered diamond dust, spreading across the ebony velvet of space, which was the suns of the Milky Way, uncountable in number, unfathomably remote. He remembered that at one time he had had a vague idea that if they could get to the heart of the Plant it might be possible to kill it. He did not know whether to laugh or cry at the absurdity of the notion. As if this radiance could be harmed . . . as if anyone could ever wish to harm it. Then the fronds opened in front of them, and he could see the full glory.

He had to turn his head away, it was so bright. But his eyes came back, irresistibly drawn, and gradually he found that he could tolerate it, and make something of the shape before him. It pulsed in a rhythm, like a heart beating, but all the time emitting the golden light in which they were both now bathed. A sort of hemisphere, rising out of a surface dark red like the fronds, a small breathing sun embedded in crimson cloth.

And yet, although he was looking at it, in a strange way he was part of it, and it of him. The radiance reached through his eyes deep into his mind. There it formed thoughts and words, which he could hear though he knew his ears played no part in the hearing.

"Welcome," the thoughts said. "Be at peace."

"We are," Steve said beside him.

He heard that through his ears; Steve had spoken aloud.

The Plant said: "We summoned you here to learn how you came to Us."

It was funny how there was the impression of real words, of an actual voice, resonant and majestic. The remark itself was more a statement than a request, assuming compliance. Somewhere inside his consciousness, Marty felt a flicker of uncertainty, a hint of refusal. This was alien, and one should be wary. It only lasted a fraction of an instant before being submerged in a new wave of conviction that there was nothing to fear or resent or mistrust. The Plant knew what was best for them and only sought to do them good. He was ready to do anything the Plant wanted, tell it anything it required to know.

But Steve was already telling the story—of their journey through the foothills to First Station, the finding of Thurgood's journal, the search for the impossible Flower and so at last the crash of their crawler through the roof of the topmost cave.

The Plant said: "Do others of your kind know of this?"

Presumably it meant had they sent a radio message back because Steve had said there were only the two of them. Steve took the same meaning, and said: "No. We weren't in touch because they would have hauled us back. We weren't supposed to take the crawler out."

The Plant would know of radio from Thurgood, of course. Thurgood would have told it about First Station, the tiny experimental outpost which, in those early days, was not expected to survive. The anti-technology riots would have been raging about the time Thurgood was lost.

"The Bubble," the Plant said. "Tell Us of that."

Steve did the telling, outlining the present size and scope of the colony, describing the mines and the observatory. Marty listened, in a happy state of relaxation. He wondered vaguely why, since it could put thoughts as verbal messages directly into their minds, the Plant did not take information from them the same way. It was probably because human thoughts were too diffuse and confused to make sense except when one consciously put them into speech. The human mind was so weak and puny altogether, compared with the wisdom of the Plant.

Steve had finished. There was a pause before the thought-words came again.

"We will care for you. Your happiness will be part of Our harmony. With Us all things are in harmony. Name your desires, and We will grant them."

Marty said: "Can you help us to get home?"

"That is impossible."

"We only need to get the crawler outside, and we'll be all right. I'm pretty sure it's undamaged.

Even if there is anything wrong, we could radio for help from the Bubble once we're in the open."

The answer was not so much a verbal statement as a sense of finality and negation. Marty still argued: "You can make trees grow anywhere you like. You could grow one under the crawler, lifting it up. And there is that hole in the roof of the cave which opens up for the Flower to go out. You could push the crawler through, with us inside."

"Impossible."

"But I don't see . . ."

He could feel that the presence in both their minds had somehow turned from him and toward Steve. The thought-voice said: "Name your desires."

Steve said: "Mr. Thurgood said that at one time there was a swimming place in the lake, with a tree to dive from. I was wondering . . ."

"It will be granted."

Negation was replaced by benevolence and assurance. It was wonderful to feel so safe, so completely protected.

The Plant said: "Be at peace in Our presence. Enjoy yourselves, nourish yourselves, in Us. We seek your happiness. For now, you may leave Us. We will summon you again at another time."

The plant-raft bobbed by the shore of the island, and moved away as soon as they were aboard. The tall fronds closed, and all that was left of the brilliance were the small lances that shone through and the column of golden light lifting to the ceiling and reflecting from it.

Marty felt confused. In his mind there was an afterglow of the protecting warmth which he had known in the presence of the Plant, but mixed now with doubts and queries. Trying to sort it out, he said to Steve: "When I asked it to get the crawler out for us and it said impossible, do you think it meant it couldn't do it, or wouldn't?"

Steve asked: "Does it matter?"

"I think so. It's the difference between wanting to help us and not."

Steve said: "It could do it if it wanted to."

"Then it's not as friendly as it seems."

"It has to protect itself," Steve said. "If news were to get back to the Bubble . . . it has no way of protecting itself. The rock is no defense against explosives and rock drills."

"Why should it need protection? Who's going to attack it?"

"People."

"I don't see why."

"Nor did the Antarctic whale."

"That was exterminated because it could be used as food."

"And don't you think someone could work out a way of using the Plant as a food supply, too? Fresh fruit for the Bubble. And fruit that keeps you young for well over half a century. I can imagine a lot of people being interested in that. Two billion of them. They'd tear the caves to bits to get hold of it."

Marty was silent for a moment. He said: "We could promise not to say anything about it."

"And do you think it could trust us? Would you, in its place?"

It was a good point. Marty said: "So we're going to get no help from the Plant, as far as getting home's concerned. In fact, it would probably try to stop us if we tried anything ourselves."

Steve said vaguely: "I suppose so."

"We've got to do something."

"There's no hurry, though, is there? We have air, water, food—everything we need."

Marty supposed he was right about that. The urgency had gone. They no longer had to depend on a dwindling supply of canned food in the crawler. They were safe from starvation. Nor was it just safety. His mouth watered as he thought of the fruit in the orchard, and he realized he was hungry. Thurgood had bundled them onto the raft without giving them time to have breakfast.

Thurgood did not ask any questions about their interview with the Plant—did not even refer to it. But he did not talk much at all; normally only when questions were put to him. Even then he was not very communicative. After they had been up to the orchard, Marty found him lying on the grass by the lake, and asked him: "When you crashed through into the caves, was your crawler damaged much?"

Thurgood remained silent, his eyes fixed on the glowing mossy ceiling. Marty repeated the question, and he finally said: "I don't think so. It's a long time ago."

That was true enough. Marty said: "Did you ever try to get out?"

"Get out?"

He seemed surprised. Marty said: "Out of the caves. To get back to First Station."

"Why would I do that?"

It was said with a genuine lack of comprehension. Marty realized that he was so accustomed to the life here that he could not contemplate any other. He remembered reading in a book once about a man who had been kept a prisoner in a small cell for twenty years, and when after that they came to let him out had begged not to be released: in the end they had to take him out by force. In Thurgood's case it was nearly four times twenty years, and instead of a cell it was a world of ease and plenty. Probably he had tried to get out at the beginning, but the idea was so unfamiliar now and unwelcome that he had forgotten ever doing so. In any case, they could not expect much help from him.

Steve, who had gone farther along the lake shore,

called Marty and he went to him. Steve said: "See that!"

The shore was no longer featureless. A tree was growing out of the grass. It was like watching a speeded-up film: you could see it, slowly but unmistakably, budding, lifting, extending. It was already a couple of feet high. And there was more than that. Under the luminous water it was possible to see that something else was growing out from the shore in a long encircling arm.

"It's making the swimming place," Steve said. "You coming in, Marty?"

Steve pulled off his clothes and waded into the water and Marty followed him. It shelved quite rapidly, and within a few feet of the shore they could lower their bodies and swim. The water was warm and buoyant—probably loaded with salts. The arm, if it grew up to the surface, would form a circle about thirty feet across. There was no real point in that, of course, but Steve had asked for it, conditioned—as Thurgood would have been before him—to the idea of artificial barriers. He trod water, looking down, and fancied that a change might be taking place at

the bottom, also. The light seemed brighter there
than elsewhere.

They swam for a time and then came out and lay
on the grass, their bodies drying quite soon in the
warm air. Thurgood had watched them for a while
but had made no suggestion of joining them. He
did not want to do anything, really, except eat and
sleep and idle about. Marty felt a chill at the
thought of becoming like that, but reminded himself how long the man had been here. They would
find a means of escape long before there was any
question of changing so: they must.

He lay and racked his brain for ideas. There was a
small rock drill as part of the crawler's equipment:
one might be able to attack the wall of the cave with
that. But one might be driving into miles of solid
rock—there was no way of knowing—and the Plant
would be aware what was happening. Thurgood had
said it was aware of everything that went on in the
outer caves, and there was no reason to doubt that . . .
Or what about somehow managing to hang on to the
bud of the Flower just before it thrust out into space,
so that one got carried out with it? That was even

more pointless than the other. The Plant would just not lift the Flower with one of them grabbing it. In any case, merely to get outside was not enough. They must have the crawler or, at least, its radio.

Eventually he gave up trying to think and let his mind drift. It was more pleasant lying and doing nothing—not even thinking very much—than he had imagined. Everything was on hand, after all: the orchard, the lake with its swimming place taking shape. He could see without moving that the tree was considerably larger than it had been. It was thickening as well as growing tall.

Steve said: "I've been thinking."

"What?"

"I wonder if we could get the Plant to grow trailing vines from the roof which we could swing on? Remember that jungle film on TV last year?"

Marty said: "I don't see why not. In one of those other caves there were plant things hanging from the roof."

"And if it grew several trees along the lake edge, we could swing from one to the other on the vines. And wind up swinging out across the lake, and dropping in."

"Yes," he said drowsily. "Sounds fun."

"We might also get the Plant to grow us an orchestra-tree that played different music. A little Mozart, maybe. And persuade it to tone down this one. I'm getting bored with marches and sickly waltzes."

He must give some more thought to escaping. But later, Marty decided. His brain felt too idle at the moment. And there was plenty of time.

Sometime during that day—they had come to think of the bright periods as day, the dark, naturally enough, as night—Thurgood disappeared again. The secret of where he went was solved, in part at least, by his return. They saw him coming in from the far reaches of the lake on the plant-raft. Steve spotted him, and drew Marty's attention.

Marty said: "I suppose he's been to the island."

"Or there could be other caves beyond."

Marty asked him when he stepped ashore. Once again he failed to answer and the question had to be repeated. He said then: "Yes, I have been to the Plant."

He spoke in an abstracted, detached voice. Marty said: "Do you talk to it? What about?"

"You would not understand."

Marty felt a familiar resentment against adults who thought because you were young you must also be dumb. He said: "Try us."

"It is not possible."

"Why not?"

"Because you are not ready."

Marty started to argue about this. Simultaneously Steve was asking when they were likely to be called to the island again, as the Plant had said they would be. They both stopped and then began again. In the middle of this confusion, Thurgood without warning dropped to the ground. It was a weird movement, seeming part conscious, part automatic. Steve said: "I think . . ."

He did not need to finish: the light was draining away, darkness falling on the cave. Marty said: "I suppose we couldn't get the Plant to leave us a night-light? Oh, well. I imagine we'll get used to it, though I'm not keen on just going out the way Thurgood does."

Steve said: "No. I feel a bit tired, though, don't you?"

"This business of light and dark," Marty said. "Thurgood said the darkness comes because the Plant withdraws into its inner self and meditates. Like someone's head being awake but the rest of his body asleep, I suppose. That means that the Plant doesn't know what's happening in the outer caves during the darkness. I suppose it must have some sort of reflexes—to reseal that cave, for instance, if something crashed through at that time—but that's probably not conscious. So if we ever do find a way of getting out we would have to take advantage of it during the darkness. And that means we really ought to have a flashlight from the crawler. Don't you think so? Steve?"

Steve very plainly was asleep.

He had told himself that he would raise the question of the flashlight first thing the next morning, but it slipped his mind. Thurgood was awake before them, and they all went up to the orchard for breakfast. One did not really get used to these fruits, Marty thought: they tasted better all the time. He wondered again about the Plant's ability to grow them. It must have got the data somehow direct from Thurgood's mind, because it was difficult to see how anyone could spell out an adequate description in words. And there was taste, too, which surely was completely indescribable. Thurgood, of course, had lived on the Earth and would remember what the tastes were like. There would have been nothing in his mind or Steve's to be read and copied.

But how was it that the Plant could read Thurgood's mind, while it needed to have Steve and him say things? Because Thurgood was older when he first came to the caves? Or through something, a sort of hypnotic closeness, which developed over the years? That seemed more likely. It could account for the way Thurgood had known the Plant wanted them to go the island. He thought he might ask Thurgood about it and, looking, saw that once more he was missing.

But it was not too difficult to find him. Marty looked and saw him on the raft, which was floating out into the lake. He told Steve, who nodded.

"Off to the island again."

"I wonder what he does there?"

"Talks, I suppose."

"What does he have to talk about, after seventy years? And he doesn't seem keen on talking to us."

"I wish he'd mentioned he was going," Steve said. "We could have got him to ask the Plant about those trailing vines."

Marty stared out across the water. The raft and Thurgood were barely visible in the shimmering haze. He must be almost at the point where the raft would turn right, carrying him to the hidden part of the lake. He said: "We could follow him."

"How? Dial another raft?"

"We could swim it. It's not far—not much more than a couple of hundred yards. And the water's warm and more buoyant than we're used to. You could always float if you got tired."

"Do you think we should?"

Thurgood might not like being followed. The Plant might not approve of their going to the island except when they were summoned. Marty decided not to brood over these possibilities. He pulled off his clothes and waded out into the lake, and after a slight hesitation Steve followed him. They swam out together. The still water foamed away from their arms and legs, leaving a faint trail of phosphorescence.

The water's buoyancy made it very easy. They turned the corner and saw the column of golden light that marked the island. There was still more light showing, a bright arc of it to one side. That would be because the fronds had parted, because Thurgood was on the island talking to the Plant. Marty had a moment's misgiving, remembering Steve's query. But it was not something which had been forbidden. Neither Thurgood nor the Plant had given any indication that there was anything forbidden here. He remembered the golden voice inside his mind: "We seek your happiness."

So they swam on toward the island. Their direction was oblique to the arc of light, but they could see it and soon see Thurgood's figure outlined against it. Marty paused, treading water. It was a posture he had not seen before except in pictures, but it could not be mistaken. Thurgood knelt before the light, head bowed, arms stretched out in supplication and self-abasement. What they were looking at was an act of worship.

10

The Hinge of Memory

THEY TURNED AND SWAM BACK IN SILENCE through the cave. In part this was due to a sense of having intruded on something private and personal; in part to shock. Marty's thoughts seemed to circle around in his head. He tried to find some other explanation for what he had seen, but could not. At last they climbed, dripping, out of the lake and sat on the grass. The tree was a lot higher, he noticed. Branches came out from it on the lake side only, at convenient intervals. Already you could see they were going to be broad and flat, making excellent diving boards. Probably springy, too, Marty thought. The Plant-God looked after its creatures.

He said: "I wonder how long he's been like that."

"Thurgood? I don't know. Years probably. Decades, maybe."

"And us?"

"What do you mean?"

Marty said: "How long before we start kneeling down and praying to it?"

"That's silly."

"Is it?"

"There's probably something wrong with him— with his mind."

"That's what they thought at First Station. They were wrong. He was sane enough."

"But after being seventy years in the caves . . ."

"All right," Marty said. "And after we've been seventy years in them?"

"We'll find a way out long before then."

"He didn't."

Steve was silent, and then said: "Perhaps he didn't try hard enough."

Marty was on the point of saying that if he did not it was probably because the Plant found a means of stopping him; when he remembered what Thurgood had said about the Plant knowing everything that went on in the caves. It could be listening to them, and it understood human speech. The time to talk was when the light went and the outer parts of the Plant slept. He tried to remember what they had just said. Nothing, he thought, that counted. The Plant would also know that they had swum out and seen Thurgood on the island, and would expect them to have a reaction to that. It would expect them to be shocked, even rebellious. What mattered was not revealing to it any plan of action they might work out.

He said: "I suppose that could be it. You're right. We'll find something."

Steve was apparently content. They lay on the grass for a while, drying off. Then Marty suggested another trip of exploration into the other caves, and Steve agreed. There was always a chance, Marty thought, that they would see something that would give them a clue to escaping, though it was a slim one. He had another motive as well. After they had explored a couple more caves, each with its quota of plant-things, he led the way up to the crawler. The moss was beginning to grow up over the tracks but had not yet got very far. Marty went inside and came out with a flashlight. He said, in case the Plant were listening: "Might as well have our own night-light since none's provided."

The day passed in idling, swimming, eating. Thurgood was back by the lake when they returned. He said nothing about the Plant or the island. He would scarcely have noticed them, with all his attention concentrated on his praying, but Marty supposed the Plant might have told him of their being there. He clearly did not want to talk, and because of that Marty pressed him. When *would* they be called back to the island?

Thurgood said: "The Plant will decide."

"Does it have to decide everything?" Thurgood looked at him blankly. "Well, does it?"

"You will learn."

"Learn what?" Marty asked. "Why the Plant

thinks it can tell us what to do and when to do it?"

Thurgood's blue eyes stared from his white face. Marty had thought he might be provoked into resentment or anger at what he would regard as impudence, maybe as sacrilege. But his reaction did not seem to be at all like that. It was more like someone in the wisdom of age listening with quiet, infinitely tolerant contempt to the foolishness of the very young. He reminded himself that Thurgood *was* very old, a hundred years old. Yet with a shiver of fear he realized that the impression was of something much more ancient than a hundred years: it seemed as though the Plant itself looked through his eyes.

Then night fell and Thurgood crumpled into sleep.

Marty said: "Steve, listen."

"I'm listening." He yawned loudly. "I'm dog tired."

"Stay awake," Marty said urgently. "We've got to talk."

"What about?"

"I was saying last night—but you'd gone to

sleep—that this is the only safe time to talk without the Plant hearing us. To find a way of escaping."

"We'll find something. We've only been here a few days."

"Look," Marty said, "when we were talking about Thurgood after we swam back from the island, you said that perhaps he didn't try hard enough. But why didn't he? He wasn't a man who gave up easily. Look at the way he stuck to the business of finding the Flower."

"Perhaps he didn't want to try. Perhaps he liked it here from the start."

"Don't you?"

"What do you mean?"

"The Plant," Marty said. "It's complete in itself. It doesn't need anything from outside. When Thurgood came in it was like a grain of sand getting into an oyster. It would be an irritant if it couldn't be neutralized, absorbed somehow. Well, he has been absorbed—or his mind has. And now there are two more grains of sand to be treated the same way. The Plant is probably getting at us already. In fact, I'm sure it is. Thurgood goes to sleep as soon as the light dims—we don't quite do that but we feel tired. It's part of the same thing."

"How is it getting at us? It didn't summon us to the island at all today."

"Perhaps that isn't important. These fruits, the water from the drinking-fountain tree—maybe the air we breathe: they could all be changing us. Remember the lotus-eaters in the *Odyssey?* They ate this fruit that made them happy and made them forget where they were or where they had come from. Isn't that what we're doing? Don't you find that the Bubble—that everything before the caves— is beginning to seem less real?"

"In a lot of ways this is better than the Bubble. No one to tell us to do things, no school. Everything we want given us."

Steve, Marty remembered, had been an orphan and a loner. There was no one he desperately wanted to see again. But even in himself he could feel the beginning of a change. He could remember his mother clearly, but his father had become a vague and distant figure.

"Everything given us so far," Marty said. "But in the end we won't want anything except to be fed and to go to the island every day and pray. Thurgood told us he had a swimming place once. It went because he no longer wanted it—no longer wanted anything except to pray to the Plant."

Steve was silent; then said: "I don't see a lot of harm in him doing that."

"Don't you? When I was talking to him just now—he wasn't really there at all. It was the Plant I was talking to. A lot of the time he's part of the Plant. At least, his mind is, which is what matters. Do you want your mind to be taken over like that, so that you only think and want what the Plant thinks and wants?"

"It's not all the time—and he's been seventy years in the caves."

"So the process is not complete yet. The Plant is in no hurry. Time doesn't exist here: Thurgood said that. It could be a thousand years before he belongs to the Plant utterly. Or ten thousand."

"Well," Steve said, "what's the rush? After five hundred years maybe we'll need to start worrying."

He was angry with Steve's obtuseness but knew he had to tread carefully, to be very, very patient. Steve had no family of his own that he missed and wanted to get back to. It was just one difference between them, but it could be a big one. In a weird way the thought of the Plant's protectiveness could be a special attraction to him—almost as though the Plant itself could represent the family he had never had.

Marty said: "In every process there's a point of no return. Like when our crawler was sliding down that slope. Nothing could stop us crashing once the slide had started. If we give in now the Plant has got us. Bit by bit we'll stop being individuals, stop having minds and wills of our own."

Steve was silent again. Marty did not know how far he was getting over to him. He pressed on: "Think about that. It's worse than the character in that book you were writing. He was chained up to a wall, but he could still think for himself. There was something to hope for—the possibility of getting free someday. Our bodies wouldn't be chained up but our minds would be. And there would be nothing to hope for because we wouldn't even want to get free. Remember the balloons? Getting punished was a proof that we were free to do what we liked. The Plant would never punish us. It would never need to."

For several moments Steve's silence continued. Marty was racking his brain for further arguments when Steve said: "You think the fruit is dangerous—that it can make us change?"

"I think it's part of it. Perhaps the most important part."

"We could stop eating it—live on the crawler rations. Only won't that make the Plant suspicious?"

"We'd better eat some, but limit it as much as possible." There was an overwhelming relief in realizing that Steve was on his side still, that they could talk about things and make plans. "We could go to the crawler at night, and fill up."

In a discouraged voice, Steve said: "The supplies won't last very long. Not seventy days, never mind seventy years."

"We don't have seventy years. In fact, if we're

still here in seventy days we're finished. We need to do something fast to have any hope at all."

"Do what? Is there any hope, anyway?"

There was another hazard, Marty realized. One could appreciate the horrifying menace of the Plant, and even so despair of overcoming it. He put all the confidence he could muster into his voice: "There's one chance. When we first met Thurgood, and he was telling us how the Plant got here and the way it worked—he said something which might help."

"What?"

"He said there were other places besides the one we fell through where the rock cover is not complete. Three or four, he said. Saying that meant he knew where they were. If one of them were in the right position, and big enough for the crawler to break through . . ."

"Small chance."

"Better than none."

"Anyway, he wouldn't tell us. You've said yourself: he worships the Plant. He won't do anything, or tell us anything, that would be against the Plant's wishes."

"He won't unless we can change him."

"How are we going to do that? Feed him canned battery-chicken roll and hope it cancels out the lotus fruits?"

"He was human once. Part of him still is, underneath. If we can make him remember . . ."

"He's not interested," Steve said. "He doesn't want to talk about anything except the Plant. He knows all his own people are dead long ago and he doesn't care about any others. When you mention the Bubble, or Earth, he doesn't want to know."

"We've got to keep at him—keep prodding away."

"But if he's gone past the point of no return, as you said—like our crawler sliding . . ."

"No return when you're on your own is not the same as no return when you've got help. If there had been a couple of other crawlers standing by and they'd been able to throw us anchors we might have made it. And he's not been taken over completely. If he's worshiping the Plant that must mean that part of him is still separate from it. You can't worship yourself."

"O.K.," Steve said. "We'll try." He sounded a bit more cheerful. "But even if we do get anywhere with him we can't make plans except at night and when night falls he flops out."

"If we can get him interested, he might not."

Steve yawned again. "I'm really beat. There's nothing we can do now, is there?"

"We could go up to the crawler and get some food."

"Not hungry."

"So we wouldn't be too hungry tomorrow, I meant."

"You go, if you like. I don't think I could face ham 'n' egg roll. I'm too tired."

Marty was tired, too. They were getting some exercise, of course, with swimming, but he felt it was not really, or not entirely, a physical tiredness. He fought it for a while, and then drifted into sleep.

The Plant said: "We understand your request, and grant it."

The boys were on the island again, having been

told by Thurgood that they were wanted. They stood in front of this brightness which seemed to have other pulsing brightnesses inside it that Marty had not noticed before. There was the same feeling of peace and benevolence, except that if anything it was stronger, surer, more all-surrounding. Notions of escape, of leaving the caves, were far-off, small, unimportant. The Plant was good, and he felt a bursting joy at the thought that it wanted to share its goodness with them. Steve had asked for the trailing vines on which they could swing out over the lake. The swimming place was nearly complete, with its firm leafy ledge running all around—you could sit on it, dangling your legs, or run along it and dive in—and the tree was over fifteen feet high, its jutting flat branches almost strong enough to bear them. Anything else they wanted would, he knew, be given them. He wanted to thank the Plant but words seemed inadequate. The Plant was so wise and great, they so puny and unimportant.

The Plant spoke to them of itself, of its own nature. Its existence was a cycle, continually self-renewing. In the caves it created forms and patterns that changed, never repeating themselves. The Plant watched its creation and delighted in it. The other part of the cycle was meditation. In this it withdrew into its inner self. Creation slept, while Mind concentrated at its deepest and most profound, withdrawn from externals and appendages and absorbed in its own glory and wonder.

All things were at harmony in the Plant. Sound had been unknown before Thurgood came—the caves had lived and flowered in eternal silence. From him the Plant had learned music, and out of the simple primitive chords which he provided it had fashioned complex glories. They too, in their small way, might contribute to this world, this universe, of joy and peace.

The spell lasted for some time after the raft took them away from the island. They sat on the grass, still dazed and overwhelmed. Thurgood had taken the raft and gone off across the lake. Marty found himself envying his freedom to go to the Plant rather than wait to be called. There was something gnawing at the back of his mind: something he had meant to do, a plan of action of some kind. But it could not be important. All that mattered was lying here in the warm scented air. The tree was still growing, and looking at the wall of the cave he could see that a vine-like plant had started climbing up from the base toward the roof. The orchestra-tree was playing Strauss again. Presumably when they had the sort of rapport with the Plant that Thurgood had they would get the kind of music they wanted. It was pleasant enough even so. Everything was pleasant because the Plant wanted them to be happy.

He did not jerk out of this mood until Steve said something about going up to the orchard. Then he remembered what they had decided the previous night: to eat as little of the fruit as possible. He said: "I'm not hungry just yet," and saw Steve remember also. They went for a swim instead, and he thought of the rest of the plan. It must wait until Thurgood returned. He scanned the lake impatiently for the returning raft.

The thought of the fruit would not go out of his head. Now that the suggestion had been made he did feel hungry, really hungry. They would have been wiser, he realized, to have eaten food from the crawler during the night, despite the effort involved in getting it. He was glad that Steve was with him in this. It made it that little bit easier.

His hunger increased as the minutes went by. It was different from any hunger he had known before, sharper and more avid. He was tantalized by the recollection of how delicious the fruits were, of their taste, their ripe juiciness. The one advantage the hunger gave was that it cleared his mind of the fog of well-being. He realized that the Plant's influence on their minds was spreading and strengthening. Time was not on their side. If they were to escape they must make the attempt soon.

At last Thurgood came back. They went to him, and talked. He was even more taciturn than usual: probably, Marty thought, because he had just returned from communion with the Plant. The questions they put, about his life before the caves, were ignored, or answered laconically and unsatisfactorily. "I don't recall." "I forget." "Maybe it was like that—I don't know."

Steve dropped out, shrugging his shoulders at the impossibility of getting anywhere. But they had to keep on, Marty thought. They had to find where the Plant's weaknesses were, and only Thurgood could help them. He continued, ignoring the silences and the brusque responses. A normal man would have got irritated by his persistence, but Thurgood was not normal. There was no place for irritability in a mind dominated by the bland euphoric calm which the Plant inspired.

In the end, he gave up questions as such but kept on talking, and talking about Earth. He talked about TV programs he had seen, ran through the plots of movie after movie, at one time found himself giving a résumé of a geography lesson on Malaysia. Thurgood lay on the grass, his eyes closed. Marty was not sure whether he was listening, whether he was awake even. Steve returned and made an effort at contributing, but soon gave it up again. Marty persisted. He was bored himself, desperately bored, and embarrassed by this monologue which he had to keep going without the least encouragement. Then a small spark ignited.

Marty had been talking about his parents, about his mother who as a girl had traveled all over the planet with her artist father. He said, as a casual afterword to this: "My father never moved out of one small town until he went to college. He was a New Englander. New Hampshire."

The first bit was something he had gleaned from his mother, during their talks following the balloon episode; his father, except that one time at the reservoir, had never mentioned his past. Thurgood opened his eyes. He said, in a remote voice: "New Hampshire? I'm from Vermont."

Marty said quickly: "What part?" Thurgood did not reply. "Were you born there?" he asked. "Did you go to school in Vermont? What was it like?"

There was no answer. It looked as though it had been merely a flicker of memory, no sooner aroused than quenched. Still he kept on, doggedly pounding away at it. He racked his mind for anything that would provide a talking point, recklessly inventing where he could not recall. He thought he was going to talk himself hoarse. His throat felt dry and the idea of an orange from the trees just up the slope was torture. But he went on and at last, very slowly, the monologue ceased to be entirely that: Thurgood was beginning to talk as well.

Steve lent a hand then, taking some of the load off him. He had thought Steve, with his imagination, would be good at this, but in fact he faltered more than Marty had done, and it was necessary to go on helping out. They prodded Thurgood into talking of anything and everything, but they found it was his childhood that gave the best response. He had been born on a farm in hill country, with fields that fitted into the lie of an old, long-inhabited land. It had been chiefly dairy farming. They had a herd of Friesians, and he remembered a tale his grandmother had told him about two of the cows: that they had been so fond of her father, his great-grandfather, that they had swum all the way from Holland when he emigrated to America. He could not have been older than four or five, and he had believed it to be true and had stared in awe at the cows, imagining their huge black and white bodies battling with the waves all the way across the vast storm-tossed ocean.

"She used to make wonderful cookies," Thurgood said, "with blobs of chocolate all the way through. And she gave me buttermilk to drink with them, pouring it out of a big blue and white jug. She said buttermilk was the best thing you could drink."

He paused. Marty was thinking of something to keep him going when he went on: "I'm getting hungry. Who's coming up to the orchard?"

It was essential to keep him in this mood of companionship. They must go with him and try to eat as little as possible. Marty was hungry, too—ravenously so. He took a banana, slowly peeled it and still more slowly started to eat. It was torture. The taste seemed even better than before, and he had to fight the impulse to gobble it down. He kept close to Thurgood, but not so close that the man would notice he was scarcely eating anything. They wandered through the orchard. Steve had been following the same technique, but Marty saw him eat an apple and then pull up one of the turnip-cheeses and nibble it. He threw him a look of warning, but Steve appeared not to notice it.

After they had eaten they went back to the lake,

and Marty continued the campaign against Thurgood. It was less successful than earlier—the fruit could have had something to do with that—but he managed to keep the tenuous link of conversation in being. Then the light faded and Thurgood, as it did so, dropped into heavy, insensible sleep.

Marty said: "I vote the first thing we do is go up to the crawler and get something to eat. I'm starving."

"There's plenty of time," Steve said. "I want to rest."

"If we rest we may go to sleep, and not wake up till it's light again. We'd better go now."

Steve said: "It's a bit pointless, anyway."

"What is?"

"Trying to get information out of Thurgood."

"He's been talking quite a lot."

"About the Earth. Not about the Plant."

"He's remembering he's human: that's what matters."

Steve said: "Look, if you did get him to a point where he was willing to tell us something, it would have to be at night, wouldn't it? And the moment the darkness comes, bingo he's out. So what's the good?"

"If we had him talking we might be able to keep him awake."

"He was talking tonight, but it didn't help."

There was no sense in arguing about it. It was their only hope and it had to be made to work. Marty said: "Anyway, are you coming up to the crawler?"

Steve yawned. "You go, if you're hungry."

Which meant that Steve was not. He must have eaten more of the fruit than Marty had thought.

He felt more despair then than he had done since the initial discovery that they were trapped. Much of this was due to the shock of realizing how much he had been depending on Steve's help— more than that, on his leadership. There had been jealousy and rivalry underlying their friendship from the start. His suggestion of taking the crawler to First Station had been caused by that. At the back of his mind had been the feeling that Steve was cleverer and stronger than he was; stronger not just physically but in character. The incident of Steve's insistence of going to look for the Flower had borne that out. He had been looking for that strength and determination now, as the factor which could just tip the balance and help them to win through. And it was not there: obstinacy and willfulness were not strength, in a case like this the reverse of it.

He said: "You won't come, Steve?"

"No. I'm too tired."

His voice was as final and uncompromising as over the hunt for the Flower. Marty knew he was on his own. He said: "O.K. I'll bring you something."

Steve did not bother to reply, or maybe he was already asleep.

He went back through the caves, lighting his way with the flashlight. It was an eerie journey. The trees were as still as though frozen. They looked gray and drab; even the fruits looked gray. The moss on the walls and ceiling, where the beam of his flashlight lighted on it, was gray, too. Color and life had been drained together as the Plant's consciousness withdrew into itself in its incomprehensible meditation.

Marty felt very much alone as he made his way along the tunnel, down the ladder tree, and through the arch to the second cave. The tree-shapes, which he had only seen threshing in motion, were as fixed as everything else, and as gray, their branches turned into stiff, lifeless tentacles. He found the rope at the bottom of the slope, and hauled himself up it, the flashlight tucked in his belt and flashing at odd angles as he swung from the rope. He reached the top and headed through the next tunnel to the top cave. The crawler lay beside the curled stem and huge bud of the Flower. He went inside, picked the first can he found in the food locker, opened it and ate ravenously.

He thought about Steve. It was important to keep him from slipping any further under the influence of the Plant. He must take some ordinary food back and get him to eat it, so that he would eat less from the trees tomorrow. But if he took it in a can the can would remain as evidence and the Plant would know they were getting food from the crawler. Even if they threw it in the lake, the Plant might know of it. One could not set limits to its awareness of the minutest details.

They must leave no traces at all, and the only way he could think of doing that was taking the food out of the can here and carrying it back in his bare hands. It was something which normally would have stood condemned on many grounds, hygiene not the least, but which answered the prime need. He picked a can whose contents seemed to be the least likely to crumble, opened it, and pried them out in a single roll.

The return journey was easier in that he was now more accustomed to the petrified night world of the caves, but had the new problem of the ham-soya roll which he had to carry. Getting down the rope was the really tricky part, but he managed it using an arm and a hand. He had to stick the flash-light back in his belt while he climbed the ladder tree one-handed, but the rest was straightforward. He came down through the orchard—even the grass was stiff as his feet brushed through, stiff and gray—and found Steve fast asleep where he had left him.

Marty put the flashlight down and shook him with his free hand. Steve mumbled but stayed asleep. He shook him again, and this time Steve turned over. As he did so, his face came into the beam of light. It was that which woke him. He blinked and sat up.

Marty gave him the ham-soya roll. He obediently took a bite, made a face, but went on eating it. Marty explained why he had taken it out of the can.

Steve said: "The taste hasn't improved."

"It doesn't matter about the taste as long as it keeps us from eating too much of the fruit."

"What's the good?" Steve said. "Thurgood will still fall asleep the moment the light goes. There's nothing you can do about that."

The flashlight lay on its side, throwing a beam of light that took in one branch of the tree by the lakeside. Marty reached out and switched it off, to conserve the battery. The idea came to him as he did so. It might work. It just might work. But it was a slim chance. He decided not to mention it to Steve. In his present mood of despondency he would only pour cold water on the whole thing.

11

The Pearl

THE DAY STARTED WELL. MARTY WOKE WITH the returning light—for the first time he saw the glow build up in the mossy roof over his head, the waters of the lake turn indigo and then blue. He watched Thurgood's slow wakening. It was more like a man emerging from a trance than from sleep, eyes opening first and seconds passing before the first movement tremored the slack immobility of his body. Marty was by him, and talking. Before night fell Thurgood had been telling an anecdote about his Dutch grandmother, and Marty picked on this. Had she really made her own cheese, in a churn?

Thurgood said: "She did. It was wonderful cheese. I never tasted anything like it anywhere else."

Not even, Marty wondered, in the turnip-cheeses that grew in the cave? But he did not want to draw Thurgood's attention in that direction. What was so good was the animation in his voice and face. Marty said: "But by herself, and a churn?"

"Well, it was powered." Thurgood smiled. "She was born in 1901, not in the Middle Ages. But she did it all herself—wouldn't let anyone lend a hand. She sold it, too, in the town. There were people who drove up all the way from New York to buy it. At least, I suppose they had other reasons for driving up, but that was the way it seemed to me as a boy. They were from New York, and they came specially to buy it: I knew that."

It was fairly easy to keep him going, by a question or a comment here and there. Thurgood wanted to talk. Now that the gate was down, reminiscence came in a flood. He spoke about the farm, his parents, relatives. There was a lot about his younger brother, David.

"He was a bit like you," he told Marty. "Not so

much in looks as in his way of talking." He smiled. "I remember a trick he had: he used to swing on my arm when he wanted something, dragging all his weight on me."

"Did you and he fight a lot?"

"No. He was five years younger. He was always getting into trouble and I was always bailing him out. There was one time he found a wild bees' nest. It was in an old stone wall and he tried to open it up, hoping to get honey from it. He was about nine at the time. I found him bawling in the lane and swarming with bees. I grabbed him and heaved us both into the pond. We came up covered in green slime and drowned bees. But Mother still had to comb them out of his hair when I got him home."

Then Thurgood remembered they had not yet breakfasted. He led the way, still talking, up to the orchard, and the boys followed. Again they ate as sparingly as possible. Thurgood tackled the fruit with his usual appetite, which inhibited conversation from his side. There was more to it than that, though. Marty noticed the silence, the noncommunication, falling on him again. When they returned to sit by the lake, the lethargy and reluctance were plain. Once more Marty's remarks were getting little or no response. All Thurgood seemed to want to do was sit and look brooding across the water.

Marty persisted, and gradually felt he was getting somewhere, starting to win him back to human memories and human feelings. The second setback was the more shattering because of this. Thurgood, almost in mid-sentence, stood up and walked to where the plant-raft floated by the shore. He made no farewell but jumped on board, and the raft took him out into the far shimmer, the haze of moss-glow and water.

The boys swam and idled while he was away. One of the tree's branches was broad and strong enough now for them to walk on. It reached out over the pool and they could dive from it. The floor of the pool was brighter than the rest of the lake and they dived down, against the buoyancy, and ran their fingers through the short silky strands that carpeted it, scattering luminosity in the water as they did so.

When Thurgood returned, the aloofness was

complete. He made no attempt to discourage them from sitting by him or talking to him, but ignored them completely. Steve drifted away after a time. Marty kept on, trying to ignore the hunger pangs which were beginning to bite. He felt he was going over and over the same ground, and wondered if he were boring Thurgood as much as he was boring himself. There was no indication, though, of even that much reaction. His body was here, but his mind was still with the Plant.

A new fear began to emerge: that the Plant would summon them again to the island. If that happened they could not refuse, and Marty remembered the overwhelming effect of their last visit. It was probable that each encounter with the Plant sapped willpower that much more. It was taking all his effort to hammer away at Thurgood: Steve had given up. To stand in that dazzling light and feel that calm, all-knowing voice echoing deep inside his mind . . . the very thought of it made him weak. Apart from that there was the possibility that the deepening of the Plant's probing and understanding of their thoughts could reveal their plan to escape. If the Plant were to ask direct questions, it might be impossible not to answer truthfully.

Against this fear, and the growing hunger for the fruits which hung from the trees only a few yards away, Marty set determination, a refusal to give in. He slogged away, battering against Thurgood's adamant silence, trying one thing after another. His grandmother was a promising subject, the younger brother another. It was the latter that, on perhaps the tenth attempt, turned the key again. Marty was saying how he went fishing with his father at the reservoir in the Bubble, and asked Thurgood if he had fished in the same way.

Thurgood said: "No." There was a pause. "My father didn't like fishing. He was an impatient man. I used to go with one of the hands. And later I took David. There was a place just across the hill where the river widened at the edge of the wood . . ."

Marty had got him going. The channel was open and he had to keep it that way. Hunger was disregarded; there was only fear that something would happen to break the continuity. As time wore by the possibility of their being called to the island lessened, but the possibility of Thurgood deciding he wanted to eat increased. There seemed to be a pattern of two trips to the orchard, after waking and not long before nightfall. He had an idea that this second one had been delayed by their talking— that Thurgood had become so engrossed in memories that he had forgotten to be hungry. But he might still choose to go, and if he did the delay would mean a much shorter time after that in which to reawaken him to humanity. He pressed on, putting up fresh questions almost before Thurgood had answered the previous ones, feverishly laying new trails for him to follow. He got him onto a long involved account of a hunting trip. Steve had caught the urgency, and was prompting with him. Then Thurgood checked, faltered, and said: "I think . . . aren't we missing supper?"

Both boys started talking at once. Watching Thurgood, Marty saw him start to say something, then hesitate. The look in his eyes . . . Was the light a fraction less bright, or was that an illusion? He grabbed the flashlight which he had kept by him, switched it on, and flashed it in Thurgood's face.

Thurgood said: "What's the idea?"

Intermittent flashes might be best. He switched the light on and off, directing it at Thurgood's eyes. Thurgood put his hand up, but the motion was one of normal reflexes and the light of the moss was now unmistakably darkening. Thurgood was protesting. Bearing him down, Marty cried: "Stay awake! Don't let go . . . You must stay awake!"

"I don't understand," Thurgood said. "What's all this about?" He looked around in bewilderment. "It's dark. I'm awake, though. I ought to be asleep. The Plant . . ."

Marty kept the light flashing. He said urgently: "We've got to talk to you. You've been conditioned to sleep as soon as darkness falls, but you mustn't. We want your help."

Thurgood said slowly: "Help? What sort of help?"

"To get out of the caves."

"Why?" Marty kept the light steady on him now; the expression on his face was one of puzzlement. "Aren't you happy here? Don't you have everything you want?"

"It's not that," Marty said. "We want to get back to our homes, our folks."

There was no point, he realized, in talking of the horror of having to submit to the Plant. Thurgood could not be expected to see that, to understand what had happened to himself. He spoke instead of how much they were missing their friends and families, and Steve rallied to him, backing him up. He watched Thurgood's face in the flashlight's beam, and saw a kind of understanding, a grudging assent.

Thurgood said at last: "I don't see how you could get out, anyway."

Steve said: "When we first met you, you said there were other places besides the top cave where the rock cover was incomplete. You can tell us where they are."

Thurgood did not answer. In his face the understanding was replaced by a blankness all too similar to the blankness he showed on returning from the island. Marty said quickly: "In the main cave—all the tunnels are on one side. Does that mean the other side is the inside of the mountain face?"

Thurgood hesitated. "Yes. That's so."

"And there are faults in it?"

"A couple. Small and high up."

"What about the cave below that? That's the lowest level of all, isn't it?"

"Yes."

"Does it have faults?"

"No, not faults."

Thurgood's tone was awkward and reluctant. Marty kept at him: "You said three or four places where the rock cover was not complete. Where are the others?"

"At the beginning . . . when the Plant was growing and developing from its seed it needed an exit channel to get rid of unwanted minerals and rocks. That was before it reached ecological balance."

"In the bottom cave?"

Thurgood nodded. Steve said: "How big?" Marty asked at the same time: "Could a crawler get through?"

"I . . . think so. Yes, it could."

Tensely Steve said: "Will you show us? We couldn't find it without you. Not in time."

"I don't know." His face gleamed in the light.

He was sweating. "The Plant would not like it."

They argued with him, in turns or together. He kept stubbornly to the same point: it was not something of which the Plant would approve. That was what mattered essentially. He understood their wanting to leave but he could not go against the Plant's wishes.

Instead of softening he seemed to become more obdurate as time went on. In the end he said, with an air of finality: "I'll talk to the Plant tomorrow. Tell it you want to leave and ask it to help. The Plant will do what's best. It only wants you to be happy."

If Thurgood did that, Marty realized, they were finished. There were a hundred different ways the Plant could stop them—ways which probably would not need to be used because each day saw them a little less able to stand out against its influence. Steve started to say something like this but Marty knew it was no good. Thurgood could not be budged by anything which might seem to be an attack on the Plant and its benevolence. It was his inner core of humanity which was important. They had reached it and they must use it. His young brother David, whom he thought Marty resembled a little . . . his trick, which Thurgood had mentioned, of swinging on his arm when he wanted something . . .

Marty passed the flashlight to Steve. He reached for Thurgood's arm, grabbed it, let his own body fall against his. He said, looking up into his face: "Help us, Andy! Help me. I'm in a jam. Get me out of here."

Thurgood stared at him. His face showed that he had seen the stratagem for what it was. He shook his head slightly. He was going to refuse, Marty thought despairingly. Then the expression softened. He said: "O.K. If it's what you really want."

They made a quick check of the crawler. It was not really adequate, but the important thing was to get moving before Thurgood had a chance to change his mind. He had been silent and preoccupied during the journey up through the caves, though the boys had kept up a running fire of talk to distract him. Now he stood awkwardly inside the crawler with a strange blank look on his face.

Steve said: "Seems O.K. You going to drive?"

"No," Marty said decisively. "You're the better driver. Set her rolling as soon as you like."

Steve got into the driving seat. Marty said to Thurgood: "She may bump on that steep slope below the tunnel. Better hang on to one of the grips."

The crawler was moving slowly forward, the cave ahead brightly outlined in its headlight beams. Thurgood had not moved, and Marty went to him and put his hand on the grip. He let it rest, but he was not holding tightly. As they lurched down the first slope into the tunnel he staggered and Marty had to help him keep his balance.

Steve held the crawler for a moment on the lip of the second descent. The beams cut a swath of brilliance through the air and lit up the roof of the cave at the far side. Marty felt uneasy. Their progress was neither visible nor audible from the island on the lake and all this part of the Plant was asleep, but he still wondered. There must be reflex action of some sort—to cope, for instance, with anything breaking through the top cave—and some level of stimulus to trigger it off. Walking through the caves at night had not done so, but two boys and a man walking was not the same as a crawler battering its way along.

He was relieved when Steve engaged the climbing spikes and the crawler tipped for the steeper descent. The lights now showed the drooping trees below, nearer and nearer as they reached the bottom. To the right there was a place where they were more thinly spread, with room to get between them. They thinned still more, and the flat expanse of fuzz was in front. They roared across it and under the arch. Avoiding a clump of the spherical bushes, Steve had to cut across the edge of the thicket of cactus-things. They loomed up, spiked and angular, and the right-hand track crunched over them. Ahead, at the bottom of this cave, was the opening to the one which Thurgood had said was the lowest in the system, the one through which, in the earliest stage of its existence, the Plant had excreted the materials for which it had no use.

The way was clear and Steve increased speed.

Something occurred to Marty as he did so, for the first time. Even if they forced a way out, there was no telling where they would be. The break could be halfway up the mountain, with a drop of hundreds of yards below. He shuddered and put the thought away. There was no point in dwelling on it.

The last cave twisted slightly to the right. They were through the opening, and Marty said urgently to Thurgood: "The weak spot—where is it?"

He hung on his arm as he did so, repeating the gesture which had worked before. Thurgood said: "Down there." He sounded dazed. "Where the cave wall recesses to the right of that outcropping."

Steve said: "I have it."

In a different voice, Thurgood said: "Wait!"

Steve stopped the crawler. "What is it?"

Marty saw what was happening. The moss was starting to glow outside the circle of the headlight beams, above and all around them.

"It's coming awake!" he said. "Push on fast."

"No," Thurgood said. He looked like a man listening to something at once far away and very close. "The Plant does not want this. The Plant wants you to stay."

Steve had set the crawler moving again. Thurgood moved toward him, hands reaching to grab. He was stronger than they were, and there were a number of ways in which he could immobilize the crawler. Marty realized that he still held the flashlight in his right hand. He was not sure whether it was heavy enough but there was nothing else to use. As Thurgood caught hold of Steve's arm, he swung the flashlight in an arc and crashed it against the back of Thurgood's head. He tottered and Marty hit him again, a more glancing blow. This time he dropped.

Steve did not look back to see what had happened. He was occupied with the controls, increasing the speed of the crawler and pointing it at the slight recess at the end of the cave.

Something else was happening: things were growing in their path. A thicket of plant tendrils was springing up from the moss, plucking at the treads which crushed through them. Could it stop them? He thought they were slowing. Then Steve hit full power and the resistance was overcome. The wall was closer and closer. It looked solid, the glowing moss that covered it no different from that anywhere around. A few yards, a yard . . .

They hit. The dazzle turned into blackness, and there was the feeling of the crawler checking against a new resistance, but one which was dragging, not solid. It lasted only an instant, and they had burst through. There was light again, but the light of the beams illuminating the weathered, arid rocks of the Moon's surface.

Steve had brakes and spikes on. The crawler slid through stone dust for maybe sixty feet before it came to a halt. They were at the top of an alley leading steeply down to a small plateau.

They were in shadow, the sun invisible behind the western peaks. Marty did not know how long they had been in the caves, but the lunar day was near its end. He looked back up the slope, and thought he saw two or three specks float and drop. He could imagine the storm of leaves inside as the Plant repaired itself.

Steve said: "We made it."

Marty nodded. "We made it."

Thurgood groaned and stirred. Marty watched him recover consciousness, clutching the flashlight. Which would it be—relief at being free of the Plant's domination or anger that they had prevented his attempt to stop them? Rejoicing, or violence? Thurgood opened his eyes and climbed unsteadily to his feet.

It was neither of those. The look on his face was one which Marty had never seen before and did not want to see again. It was a look of utter desolation and loss, the expression of someone who has only one reason for living and is watching it die. He said, in a whisper: "Let me go back."

"You're all right now," Marty said. "They'll look after you in the Bubble. They'll do things for you."

Thurgood said: "You don't understand. You can't begin to imagine what it was like. The wisdom, the splendor of the Plant. I could not begin to tell you."

Steve switched on the reverse beam. It lit up the powdery slope down which they had slid; above that the rock face. There was a concavity in it which might have been the spot they had broken through, but it looked no different from anywhere else on the side of the mountain.

Steve said: "It's sealed itself. You can't go back."

Thurgood did not answer. His face had the air of attention, of listening, which Marty had noticed when the moss started to glow. Could the Plant reach his mind out here, or was this the last flickering of an old compulsion? Thurgood unhooked one of the spacesuits, and started to climb into it.

Steve said: "No!" He looked at Marty. "We must stop him."

If the Plant could still reach him, he could be dangerous. It would not be so easy to knock him out a second time. And there was a long journey ahead, back to the Bubble. Marty said: "Let him go if he wants to."

It was a sign, Marty supposed, of the ascendancy he had acquired over Steve that he did not argue; but how little that mattered now. Thurgood zipped up the suit, and went through into the airlock. He said nothing to the boys. Marty wanted to thank him for helping them, but there was nothing he could say which had any meaning against the grief and longing in the man's face. There was the hiss of air, and Thurgood appeared outside, slipping and sliding as he toiled upward.

"What's the good?" Steve asked. "He can't get in."

"We couldn't have stopped him."

"When he finds it's hopeless . . . he might open the valves."

And if he did, Marty thought, would it be so much more terrible than carrying that misery through a world in which every soul he had known was dead and gone? Splendor, Thurgood had said. Something they could never understand, that he could not begin to explain. It might be so. When the grain of sand entered the oyster, the oyster smothered it to protect itself; but what resulted was a pearl.

He watched as Thurgood reached the rock face, and leaned against it. He did not want to witness the man's agony and turned away. It was Steve's cry of astonishment which pulled him back.

In time to see that which looked like rock incredibly splitting, to see Thurgood forcing his way through against the outward rush of air, and to see the way closing behind him as he re-entered his paradise.

Steve asked: "What are we going to tell them when we get back?"

It was a big question. They had discovered something which would excite the whole of mankind: the first alien life, alien intelligence. Instead of being punished they would be made much of. The scientists would listen attentively to every word they spoke. They would be asked to pinpoint the mountain on the lunar map, perhaps even to accompany the expedition that would be launched, as soon as possible, to make a full exploration and investigation.

And then? Rock drills ripping through into the living being of the Plant? Testing laboratories set up in the lake cave, analyzing the fruits that might enable men to live forever? They would probably try to do as little damage as possible—the days of slaughtering the dodo to extinction were over— but it would make no difference. The Plant had absorbed one irritant, and could have absorbed two more. But it could not absorb scientists and their instruments, all the power and curiosity of Man. Its aeons-long life would gutter away in death.

It had tried to assimilate them to itself but only because it could not do otherwise. Afterward, when they were free, it had called Thurgood back but had not bidden him destroy these witnesses to its existence and its hiding place. For all its wisdom and age and might it was vulnerable, defenseless against evil.

Marty said: "Nothing. We went out in the crawler, took a look at First Station, explored around. That's all."

Steve said: "They may check our supplies. We won't have used as much oxygen and food as we should."

"We'll work it out roughly and ditch that amount. We'd better ditch Thurgood's diary, too."

"And we're a suit short."

"We damaged it, and left it behind somewhere."

"Will they believe that?"

"What else can they believe? That we last saw it

on a hundred-year-old man who walked into a mountain?"

Steve said, with resignation: "We're heading back into a load of trouble."

"Yes." Marty grinned. "It doesn't last, though. And the sooner we hit it, the sooner it's over. You drive, I'll map-read."

The crawler started on down the slope. They reached the plateau and he looked up to see the misty globe of Earth overhead. He thought of Thurgood inside the mountain, making his way through his beloved caves to the lake and the island, and the bright pulsing light that beamed from it. When he himself was an old, old man Thurgood would still be there, unchanged, eating the fruits that never cloyed, worshiping the beauty and wisdom of the Plant.

He was glad to be free, glad to be on his way home, but there was a glimmer of something underneath the gladness. Only a hint of a feeling, but he wondered if it could be envy.

Read on for a peek at John Christopher's epic dystopian adventure novel!

THE PUBLIC LIBRARY WAS IN A QUIET, GLOOMY street facing the park. It was joined on to rambling dilapidated buildings which had been council offices but were currently used as a warehouse. The library itself was almost as old—a plaque coming away from the wall told of an opening ceremony in 1978—and crumbling badly. There were several large cracks in the concrete surface, once white, now a dirty gray streaked with black.

The interior was not much better. The artificial light supplementing what little filtered in on this dull April afternoon came not from lumoglobes but from antiquated fluorescent tubes. They flickered and hummed; one was dead and another spasmodically blanked and brightened. The librarian, sitting behind his desk, showed no sign of being aware of this. He was a tall, stooping man with a high, domed forehead and a limp white moustache which he continually fingered.

He was a taciturn man, not talking to borrowers except insofar as was absolutely necessary. Once, a couple of years ago, he had engaged Rob in conversation—that was some months after Rob's mother died. Rob had gone to the library in the first place along with her and then had continued on his own. The librarian had said how he had worked here since leaving school, nearly fifty years earlier, and had told him that in those days he had been one of six assistants. There had even been a project for moving to a new, larger building and taking on more staff. It was four decades since that had been abandoned and now he did everything himself. He was past retiring age but stayed because he wanted to. The council talked of closing the library and pulling the building down; meanwhile, they let things run on.

He talked in a half melancholy, half angry way of the virtual disappearance of reading. In his young days there had been no holovision, it was true, but there had been television. People had still read books. People had been different then; more individual, more inquiring. Rob was the only person under fifty who came to the library.

The librarian had looked at Rob with a hopefulness, a hunger almost, that Rob found alarming and embarrassing. To him the library was associated with memories of his mother. He read books because she had, though not the same sort. Both kinds were about the past, but she had liked love stories with country settings. Rob preferred adventures: excitement and the clash of swords. He had read *The Three Musketeers* and its sequels, *Twenty Years After* and *The Vicomte de Bragelonne,* half a dozen times.

He had responded awkwardly and unwillingly to the librarian's remarks and the old man, discouraged, had returned to his customary silence. On this afternoon he stamped his books and dismissed him with a nod. Rob stayed for a moment in the lobby, looking out. The sky was darker than when he had arrived, threatening heavy rain. It was a short walk to the bus stop but a much longer one at the other end; their home was some distance from the nearest route. The stadium, on the other hand, was as near, and his father's duty shift ended within an hour. He could wait and go home with him in the car.

So instead of going away from the park, he crossed it. It was a poor place. There were unkempt flower beds and battered, sickly looking trees around the edges, budding with unpromising leaves. The rest, apart from the children's playground in one corner and a number of football goal posts, was twenty-five acres of scuffed grass and mud, crossed by half a dozen pitted tarmac paths. It did provide, though, a sense of being free of buildings. From the center one could see, above the lower near skyline, the high-rise blocks that stretched out across the sprawl of Greater London to the distant Green Belt dividing this Conurb from the next.

Half a dozen young children were playing and shouting on the swings and roundabouts. A few people were also walking dogs in the park. There were more in the short road leading to the High Street, and the High Street itself was fairly full. Not just with shoppers, he realized, but with the crowd beginning to come away from the afternoon session of the Games. They seemed reasonably orderly, and there had been no real trouble for several weeks—not since the big riot in February.

Rob turned into Fellowes Road, against the stream. It was not long after that he heard a shout from in front, followed by ragged chanting.

"Greens! Greens!"

There were other confused, indistinguishable cries and he became conscious of a tremor, a change of pace, in the mob of people coming toward him. Someone broke into a run, then others. Rob looked for cover and found none. This was a street of old, terraced houses, doors opening directly on the pavement. It was not far to the intersection with Morris Road, and he made an effort to squeeze through that way. But from one moment to the next the crowd solidified, turning into a struggling, shouting battering ram of humanity that lifted and crushed and carried him away.

He remembered that the program that afternoon had been terraplaning. In this, electrocars raced around the high-banked sides of the arena, running almost to vertical directly under the stands, and were boosted by auxiliary rockets at intervals so that they took off and flew through the air. Accidents were frequent, which was one of the things that made the sport popular with spectators. And enthusiasm was roused to a point that could fan the antagonism always present between the four factions—Blacks, Whites, Greens and Reds—to fury. Greens had been dominant in terraplaning for some time. It might be that there had been an upset, or a particularly bad piece of fouling.

He had neither time nor inclination to think much about this. His face was wedged against a brown overcoat, the cloth rough and fusty smelling. Pressure was increasing and he found it difficult to breathe. He remembered that in the February riot eight people had been crushed to death, in the one just before Christmas more than twenty. He had a glimpse of a corner of a building and realized they had spilled out into the High

Street. There was a crash of metal somewhere, people screaming, the bleep of horns. Pressure relaxed slightly; he could move his arms and one foot touched the ground. Then someone or something tripped him and he fell. Someone trod on his arm, someone else, agonizingly, in the small of his back.

Unless he did something he was finished. He could see, indistinctly, through a man's legs, a car which had been brought to a standstill. He forced a way, getting a couple more kicks before he reached it. Then he slid under—there was just enough clearance—and lay there, numb and bruised, watching the torrent of legs and feet and listening to the wild screams and shouts.

Gradually it slackened and ebbed, and at last he could crawl out and stand up. There were several people in the road lying still, others moving and moaning. Two police copters were on the scene, one parked, the second hovering some distance down the street. There were a man and woman in the car under which he had sheltered; its front wing, he saw, had been bent in by pressure. The woman opened a window and asked Rob if he was all right. Before he could do more than nod, the man had set the car in motion, and it drove away, swerving to avoid bodies and other vehicles. Several cars had been turned over and a couple were in nose-to-nose collision.

A hospital copter arced down over the nearby roofs and more were approaching. Rob went to look for his library books which had been torn from his grasp in the rush. He found one in the gutter at the corner of Fellowes Road, the other ten yards farther up. It was open and had been trodden down: there was a heel mark deeply impressed on one page and another was torn almost across. He pressed it back into shape as best he could, tucked both books under his arm, and headed for the stadium.

The stadium was nearly half a mile long and rose three hundred feet in the air, an oval of dull gold unbroken on the outside. A few people were still coming away from the nearest exit gate and cars were issuing from the below-ground parking places, but the main rush was over. Rob went to a service entrance and showed his disk to the scanner. It was a duplicate which his father had obtained for him; strictly speaking they were only on issue to staff but the rule was not taken seriously. The door hissed open and closed behind him when he had gone through. He turned right along the panel-lit corridor, heading for the main electrical section. He would not be allowed into any of the control rooms, but he could wait in a leisure room.

Before he reached it, though, he saw someone he knew. It was at the point where several corridors intersected and the man crossed just ahead of him. Rob called, and he stopped and waited for him to come up.

It was Mr. Kennealy, a friend of his father, also an electrician. He was a stocky, slow-speaking man with a broad face and very black hair. He never showed much emotion but Rob thought he had an odd look now.

"Did they tell you, then, Rob?"

"Tell me what, Mr. Kennealy? I thought I'd go home with Dad." Mr. Kennealy was studying him and Rob became aware of his dirty and disheveled appearance. "There was a riot over toward the High Street. I had to get under a car. . . ."

"There's been an accident," Mr. Kennealy said quietly.

"To do with . . . ?"

He did not want to finish the sentence. Apprehension made his throat dry.

"They've taken your father to the hospital, Rob. He got hold of a live wire by mistake. He was pretty badly shocked before anyone could switch off."

"He's not . . ."

"No. But he'll be away for a while. I was wondering how to get a message to you. I think you'd better stay with us for the time being."

They lived in a high rise overlooking the stadium and only a few minutes' walk away. He had been there many times with his father and liked Mrs. Kennealy, a large, red-faced woman, strong armed and heavy handed. It was much better than the thought of going back on his own to the empty apartment.

"Can I go to see him in hospital?"

"Not today. There's visiting tomorrow afternoon." Mr. Kennealy glanced at his finger-watch. "Come on. I'll take you back. I can clock off early for once."

They walked over in silence: Mr. Kennealy did not say anything and Rob was not eager to talk either. He was not only shocked by what had happened but confused. His father had got hold of a live wire . . . but he had always been so careful, checking and double-checking everything. He wanted to ask Mr. Kennealy about it, but he felt that to do so would be a sort of criticism.

Two of the three lifts in the block were out of order and they had to wait some time to be taken up. Mr. Kennealy complained of this to his wife, who came out of the kitchenette as they went into the tiny hall of the apartment. Maintenance was terrible and getting worse.

"You'll have to look at the HV, too," Mrs. Kennealy added. "It's gone wrong again. You're back early. I see you've got Rob with you. Is Jack coming up later?"

He told her briefly what had happened. She came to Rob, put an arm across his shoulders and gave him a squeeze. He was aware of looks passing between them which he could not read, and was not sure he would have wanted to.

"I've got the kettle on. Go and sit down, the pair of you, and I'll bring you some tea."

In the sitting room the holovision set was blaring away, showing a soap opera. The figures were hazy, occasionally switching from three- to two-dimensional, and the colors were peculiar. Mr. Kennealy cursed and, after switching off, removed the back and started tinkering. Rob watched him for a time and then went to the kitchenette. There was barely room for anyone else when Mrs. Kennealy was there.

"What is it then, Rob?" she asked.

"I was wondering if there was anything I could mend this book with. There's a page torn."

"Books." She shook her head. "What do you want with them, anyway? Well, I suppose it takes all sorts. There's some sticky tape somewhere. Yes, on that top shelf."

Rob put the torn edges together and carefully taped them. Watching him, she asked him how it had got in such a state, and he told her about the riot.

"Hooligans. There's too much of it altogether," she said. "They ought to put them in the army and send them out to China."

The war in China had been going on as long as he could remember. Troublemakers were sometimes given the option of enlisting and going out there instead of to prison. It was all far away and unreal. She had said it perfunctorily, her mind more on making the tea. Now she gave him a tray, with teapot and cups and saucers and a plate of chocolate biscuits.

"Take this through while I wipe up," she told him. "I'll be along in a minute."

Mr. Kennealy was still fiddling with the inside of the HV set. Rob put the tray down on a coffee table and went over to the window. The long-threatened rain had come and was sheeting down the chasm between this block and the next to the dark gloomy street hundreds of feet below. He stood watching it, thinking of his father and feeling miserable.

. . .

The apartment had a spare bedroom, once used by the Kennealys' daughter, who had married and left home. Rob was put up there, in a pink bed patterned with roses. He read for a time and then, tired, thumbed out the light and was soon asleep.

He woke again, feeling thirsty, and made for the bathroom to get a drink of water. He went very quietly, imagining it was the middle of the night and not wanting to disturb anyone, but heard voices as he crossed the lobby and noticed a line of light under the sitting-room door. Men's voices, three at least. They seemed to be arguing about something. Coming back quietly from the bathroom he heard his father's name mentioned, and stopped to listen. He could only catch a word here or there—not enough to get the sense of what was being said. He realized how bad it would look if someone were to come out and find him eavesdropping, and went back to bed.

He did not sleep, though. He could hear the low murmur of voices through the wall and found that he was straining to listen to them. Then after what seemed a long time there was the sound of a door opening, and the voices louder and clearer in the lobby outside.

A man said: "There's something wrong. I told him a week ago he needed to watch out."

"Accidents happen," another voice said.

"You can't take chances," the first voice insisted. "I'd warned him. You have to take account of the risks. This is a dangerous business. We'd all better remember that. Not just for ourselves but for the others, too."

"Quiet," Mr. Kennealy said. "The boy's in there. And the door's ajar."

There were footsteps and the door was gently shut. Rob heard their muted voices for a few more moments before the two visitors took their leave and Mr. Kennealy went to his bedroom. Rob lay awake still, thinking about what he had heard. He was angry at the things the men had said, the first speaker anyway. He was not only blaming his father for what had happened, but suggesting that he had put others at risk. How could that be true, when it was just a matter of touching a wire that was live when he thought it was insulated?

And Mr. Kennealy . . . he had stopped the man, but only because he had thought Rob might hear. He had not stood up for his father as he ought to have done. Rob was hating him, too, as he finally fell asleep.

The hospital was a fairly new building, more than forty floors high, its exterior in pale-green plasti-brick with anodized aluminum trim on the windows. The windows gleamed brightly in spring sunshine—the sky was blue except for a few white clouds in the west. At the very top was the balcony ringing the roof garden and heliport, toward which an ambulance copter was at this moment dropping. The doctors also parked their copters up there, coming in from the County, but there would be few at present. Only a skeleton staff remained on duty on Sunday.

The Kennealys and Rob joined the queue of people waiting for the lifts, which did not operate until the start of visiting hour. At least, this being a hospital, they were all working. They were whisked up quickly and into a second line of people waiting outside the ward door. A bored medical clerk, his head tonsured in the latest fashion, checked off names on a list. When they reached him, he said, "Randall? Not down here. You must have come to the wrong ward."

"We were told F.17."

"They're always getting things wrong," the clerk said indifferently. "You'd better go and ask downstairs."

Mr. Kennealy said in a quiet but hard voice, "No, you call them up. We're not wasting time going all the way down there again on your say-so."

"The procedure . . ."

Mr. Kennealy leaned over the desk. "Never mind the procedure," he said. "You call them."

The clerk obeyed sullenly. He did not use the visiphone but his handphone. They heard but could not make out the tinny whisper of speech at the other end. The clerk asked for a check on Randall, J., admitted the previous afternoon. He said: "Yes, got that," and replaced the phone.

"Well," Mr. Kennealy said, "where is he?"

"In the morgue," the clerk said. "He was taken

into Intensive Care this morning and died of heart failure."

"That's impossible!" Mr. Kennealy said.

His face was white, Rob saw, while the shock hit him too. The clerk shrugged. "Death's never impossible. They'll give you particulars at the office. Next, please."

Mrs. Kennealy came with Rob to help sort things out. She clucked over the untidiness and set about putting the place to rights while Rob packed his clothes and belongings. The furniture, he supposed, would be sold. He wondered if it would be possible to keep the saddle-backed chair in which his mother used to sit in the evenings. He would have to ask Mrs. Kennealy if she could find room for it, but did not want to bother her at the moment.

He left her cleaning and rearranging the living room and went into his father's bedroom. The bed was made, but a towel had been left lying carelessly across the foot, and two bedroom slippers were at opposite ends of the rug. There was a half-empty pack of cigarettes on the bedside table, a glass with a little water in it, and the miniradio which his father had sometimes listened to at night. He remembered waking and hearing the sound of music through the dividing wall.

He still could not properly grasp what had happened. The suddenness was as shocking as the fact. His mother had been continuously ill for a long time before she died—he could scarcely remember a time when she was not ill. Her death had been no less horrifying for that, but even then, when he was ten, he had known it to be inevitable. His father, on the other hand, had been a strong, active man, always in good health. It was impossible to imagine him dead. He could not be.

Rob opened the wardrobe. The clothes would probably be sold, too—they would fit Mr. Kennealy. He felt his eyes sting, and pulled open one of the drawers at the bottom. More clothes. A second drawer. Folded pullovers, and a cardboard box. On the outside was written "Jenny," his mother's name. He took it out and opened it.

The first thing he saw was her photograph. He had not known one existed: he remembered his father once trying to get her to have a photograph taken, and her refusal. This was an old-fashioned 2-D print, and it showed her as much younger than he had known her—scarcely more than twenty, with brown hair down her shoulders instead of short as she had worn it in later years.

He looked at it for a long time, trying to read behind the slight, anxious smile on her face. Then he heard Mrs. Kennealy calling him. He had time to see that there were other things in the box—a curl of hair in a transparent locket, letters in a bundle held together by a rubber band. He closed the box and put it with his own things before going to see what Mrs. Kennealy wanted.

Rob was called from geography to the principal's office. They were without a master at the time, though of course under closed-circuit TV observation at the main switchboard; and the holovision set was taking them on a conducted tour of Australia, with a bouncing, breezy commentary full of not very funny little jokes. The voice blanked out though vision continued, and with a warning ping a voice said, "Randall. Report to the principal immediately. Repeat. Randall to the principal's office."

The commentary came up again. One or two of the boys made their own even less funny jokes about possible reasons for his being summoned, but Mr. Spennals was on the switchboard that morning and the majority kept their attention firmly on the screen; he was not a man to trifle with.

Assemblies apart, Rob had seen the principal twice before; once when he joined the school, the second time when they met in a corridor and he was given a message to deliver to the masters' common-room. He looked at Rob now as though wondering who he was. This was not surprising since there were nearly two thousand boys in the school. He said, "Randall," tentatively, and then more firmly, "Randall, this is Mr. Chalmers from the Education Office."

The second man was broad where the principal was thin, with hairy cheeks and a quiet watchful expression. Rob said, "Good morning, sir," to him, and he nodded but made no reply.

"Mr. Chalmers has been looking into your case, following the regrettable death of your father," the principal said. "You have only one close relative, I understand, an aunt living in"—he glanced at a pad in front of him—"in the Sheffield Conurb. She has been consulted. I'm afraid she does not feel able to offer you a home. There are difficulties—her husband is in poor health. . . ."

Rob said nothing. It had not occurred to him that this would even be suggested. The principal continued, "Under the circumstances it is felt that the best solution to your problem—in fact the only solution—will be to have you transferred to a boarding school where you can have full care and attention. We feel . . ."

Rob was so surprised that he interrupted. "Can't I stay with the Kennealys, sir?"

"The Kennealys?" The two men looked at each other. "Who are they?"

Rob explained. The principal said:

"Yes, I see. The neighbors who have been looking after you. But that would not be suitable, of course, for the longer term."

"But they have a spare room, sir."

"Not suitable," the principal repeated in a flat, authoritative voice. "You will be transferred to the Barnes Boarding School. You are excused classes for the remainder of the day. Transport will be sent to pick you up at nine o'clock tomorrow morning."

Rob took the bus to the stadium where he knew Mr. Kennealy was on duty. On the way he thought about the State boarding schools. Some were supposed to be not quite so bad as others, but they were all regarded with a mixture of contempt and dread. They catered to orphans and the children of broken marriages, but also to certain types of juvenile delinquents. There were ugly rumors about the life there, particularly about the terrible food and the discipline.

Rob sent in a message asking for Mr. Kennealy, who came out to the leisure room ten minutes later. Rob had been watching the closed-circuit holovision which showed what was happening in the arena. It was gladiators in high-wire combat. In this, men fought with light, blunt-ended fiberglass spears from separate wires that approached each other at differing heights and distances. The wire system was complex and changed during the contest. The drop could be into water or onto firm ground, which in this case was covered with artificial thorn bushes, glinting with murderous-looking spikes. A loser always got hurt, sometimes badly, occasionally fatally. There were three men in the present fight and one had already fallen and limped away with difficulty. The remaining two swayed and probed at each other in the bluish light cast by the weather screen which at the moment covered the top of the stadium.

"Well, Rob, what are you doing away from school?" Mr. Kennealy asked.

Rob told him what had happened. Mr. Kennealy listened in silence.

"They said I couldn't stay with you, but it's not true, is it?"

Mr. Kennealy replied heavily, "If that's what the regulations say, there's nothing we can do."

"But you could go and see them—you could apply for me."

"It wouldn't do any good."

"There was a boy at school last year—Jimmy McKay. His mother went off and his father couldn't manage. He went to Mrs. Pearson in your block and he's still living there."

"The Pearsons may have adopted him."

"Couldn't you? Adopt me, that is?"

"Not without your aunt giving consent."

"Well, she won't have me herself. She's said so."

"That doesn't mean she'd be ready to sign you away. She might be thinking things will change later, that she can take you then."

"They could ask her, couldn't they? I'm pretty sure she'd say yes."

"It's not as easy as that." Mr. Kennealy paused and Rob waited for him to go on. "What I mean is, this may be the best thing for you. You'll be safer there."

"Safer? How?"

Mr. Kennealy started to say something, then shook his head.

"Better looked after. And with boys of your own age. Mrs. Kennealy and I are too old for a boy like you to have to live with."

"You said 'safer.'"

"It was a slip of the tongue."

There was a silence. Mr. Kennealy was not meeting Rob's eyes. Rob felt he could see the truth of the matter. All these were excuses, attempts to conceal the central fact: the Kennealys did not want him. He felt a bit as he had when Mr. Kennealy had not spoken up for his father against the man who had said that he was to blame for getting killed, but now it was more a feeling of desolation than anger.

"Yes, Mr. Kennealy," Rob said.

He had turned away. He found himself grasped by the shoulders, and Mr. Kennealy stared into his eyes.

"It's for your good, Rob," he said. "Believe that. I can't explain, but it's for your good."

Inside the holovision screen one figure lunged, the other parried and struck back and the first dropped ludicrously on his back, into the thorns. Rob nodded. "I'd better go back and see about packing my things."

**Read on for a peek at another exciting
adventure novel by John Christopher!**

I AWOKE WITH THE EARLY MORNING SUN DAZ-
zling my eyes. This was not in itself unusual
because my window faced east, but it triggered
a sense of something being wrong. There had been
a bothering light in my eyes the night before, from
the full moon, and in the end I had climbed out of
bed and drawn the curtains against its brilliance.
Yet they were open now.

That was when I remembered the nightmare. I'd
had nightmares before, when I was little—I could
call up hazy recollections of smoke and fire and
fear—but there had been nothing like that for

years. I had slept, in those days, in a cot beside
Mother Ryan's bed, and been lifted in beside her to
be comforted. Last night, too, Mother Ryan had
provided comfort, but she must have come the
length of the corridor to reach me. She had sat on
the edge of my bed, trying to persuade me there was
nothing to be frightened of. In the end, she had left
me and gone to the window and opened the curtains
to show me there really was nothing out there but
moonlight. Even then I had taken some convincing.

It had seemed so real! And yet it was a reality
without shape. I had known there were things outside but could not tell what sort of things they
were. All I was conscious of was that howling, ebb-
ing, and swelling as they circled the house. Each
time it died down I thought they might be going
away, but each time they came back and there
seemed to be more of them than before.

My one concern was to escape—hide under the
bed, or better still run and find somewhere in the
house where I could not hear them. But I could not
even sit up; my legs refused to move, and a dead
weight pinned my shoulders. Then the shapeless

voices stopped circling and were wailing monstrously against my window. Glass could not hold against such a volume of sound . . . and as I thought that, it shattered, and I knew they were in the room with me.

I suppose that was when I started yelling, still not knowing what they were and not daring to look. It seemed a long time before Mother Ryan was beside me, telling me to hush, it was only a bad dream—urging me to open my eyes and see there was no one there but her—no sounds except those of the distant sea and the wind in the pines, and her voice, part chiding but more reassuring.

"It's Andy's the cause of it, the little-good-for. He was at the Master's brandy again yesterday, and when the liquor's in him his tongue flaps nonsense. But I'm astonished at you paying heed to him. You should be used to his blather."

Had I been thinking clearly, it would have surprised me too. I'd known he was drunk when he came in, from his careful stiff way of walking. I hadn't believed a word of his ramblings about the black Demons, and the way they winged across the night skies, hunting for sinners—children especially—to take back to their lairs in the moon. Paddy and I had laughed about it after he'd gone, over our bedtime milk and biscuits.

"There's all manner of things happen," Mother Ryan said, holding me close, "over on the mainland. We know little about them, nor need to. They've nought to do with the Western Isles. There's no cause to fear Demons here. You know that, Ben, you know it well."

She must have stayed with me till I fell asleep. Wide awake in daylight, I writhed at the thought. If the noise I'd made had been loud enough to rouse her, Paddy might have heard it too. And Antonia. I visualized the little twist that lifted a corner of Antonia's mouth when she was hiding a smile—or pretending to.

Paddy and Antonia were Mother Ryan's daughters—no kin to me but, since I had lived with them all my life, almost like sisters. Elder sisters: Paddy by eighteen months, Antonia more than four years. Antonia was tall and thin, with fair hair that until recently had been kept tied back in a bun but was now let down, falling to the middle of her back. She had sharp gray eyes, quick and impatient movements. When she was angry it was in a held-back way more alarming than Mother Ryan's hot bursts of temper.

I doubt if anyone would have taken her and Paddy for sisters. Paddy was more sturdily built and ruddier; she had blue eyes, thick black hair cut short, and a much greater inclination to talk and laughter. We fought quite a lot because she had a bossy streak, but we did nearly everything together. I could not imagine life without her, though for that matter it was impossible to imagine life without any of the people among whom I had grown up—Mother Ryan, Antonia, Andy, and Joe, even the remote forbidding figure of the Master.

That morning, after we had our own breakfast, Paddy and I went down to the little paddock to give Jiminy his. Jiminy was a horse, swaybacked and nearly blind, who had been put out to grass. We took him his favorite snack—a sandwich with jam from last summer's plums—and he performed his usual trick of whinnying when he saw us coming, then backing away and circling before returning to the fence, yellow teeth bared in a greedy grin.

We went through the routine of feeding him and stroking his still velvety muzzle, but it wasn't the same. There had been an awkwardness over breakfast, and it persisted. Eventually I moved away toward Lookout, the highest point on the island, with Paddy following. Apart from a bank of cloud far off in the east and a few small clouds on the western horizon, the sky was blue, the air warm and carrying scents of spring.

From Lookout one could see all the other islands. Sheriff's, the only one with more than two score inhabitants, lay southeast across the central bay. John's and Stony were to our left; to our right, Sheep Isle and West Rock and January completed the ragged arc. Some of the names were self-explanatory: Stony was stony indeed, the green turf of Sheep was studded with white shapes, and it was from Sheriff's that Sheriff Wilson governed all the isles except the one on which we stood. This was Old Isle—I didn't know why except that it had a ruin much older than those on Sheriff's, which we knew were left over from the Madness. It was built with stones that bore the marks of hundreds, perhaps thousands of years of weathering.

We had explored all the islands, summer by summer. At one time we had been obliged to rely on Joe to take us, but since the previous spring we'd had the use of a small dinghy and could, with Mother Ryan's permission, roam freely. We had planned to camp a night on John's during the coming weekend.

Paddy chattered while we looked out—about when Liza, the tortoiseshell cat, might have her kittens; about Bob Merriton, who had come over from January to court Antonia but been quickly mocked into a shamefaced retreat; about the school of seals Joe said had come into the bay on the far side of Stony. But her chatter had an uncertain note, and as is likely to happen with people who are using words to fill an awkwardness, in the end she ran out of them. The silence that followed was heavy. She broke it with a yawn.

"I don't know why I feel tired. I slept like a log last night."

The yawn was too obvious, but I would have known she was lying anyway—and why. I said curtly, "Better go back to bed, in that case."

I walked away, but she came after me. "I'm sorry, Ben."

"What about?"

She was silent again but continued to follow as I walked down the hill. At last she said, "I get frightened, when I think about them. I know there aren't any here, but that's not to say they might not come one day. There's no telling how far they can fly."

I swung round to face her. "So you did hear me yelling, in the night!" She made a movement of her head that could have been a shake or a nod. "It was a nightmare, that's all. Anyone can have a night-mare."

It was definitely a nod this time. "I know."

"When I'm awake I'm not scared of them."

"Well, I am. I'm glad we live where there aren't any."

I knew she was trying to make things right, and while I still nourished resentment, I was happier.

However much we fought, I could be sure of Paddy being basically on my side. And there was some relief in having it in the open.

I said, "I wonder *why* they don't come here. Perhaps they can't fly over water."

"Mother said they had them in Ireland, and that's across water from the rest of the mainland. Maybe they don't think there's anything in the Isles that needs punishing." She thought about that. "Or perhaps we're too far off, too unimportant."

"Or they're scared of the Master."

Paddy laughed, but it wasn't entirely a joke. It was hard to imagine even Demons taking on the Master. We had come to the ruins, and a couple of early butterflies—clouded yellows—waltzed overhead, spiraling up past a pillar of crumbling gray stone.

"Do you want to talk about it," Paddy asked, "the nightmare?"

"No."

I was certain of that. Discussing Demons in an abstract way was one thing. I couldn't begin to talk about the howling and my impotent panic. Awkwardness started to come back.

Paddy said, "I was thinking . . ."

"What?"

"Liza's kittens—she had her last litter in the old pigsty. I wonder if she's gone back there?"

I said more cheerfully, "She might have. We could go and look."

Later that day Andy brought me disturbing news: I was to accompany the Master on his customary afternoon ride around the island.

On my previous birthday, the Master had surprised me by giving me a present, in the shape of a pony. He had not previously marked such occasions for any of us. There always was a present which was supposed to be from the Master, but we knew Mother Ryan had made it or got it from Sheriff's and wrapped it up before putting the Master's seal on it.

And a pony was something special. Joe had brought it across secretly the night before, but the Master himself summoned me to the paddock and handed me the reins. He didn't say much, only, "So you're fourteen, boy. On the mainland, they would call you a man." Then, without waiting for thanks to emerge from stammering confusion, he turned and walked away.

Antonia had just been scornful; for two or three days afterwards she greeted me by dropping her voice and saying, "On the mainland, they would call you a man." I don't think she minded my being given the horse; she was not fond of animals and shooed the cats away if they ventured into the parlor.

Paddy, though, had been resentful at first, pointing out that all she'd had for becoming fourteen was a new hat. But she got over it quickly, principally by treating the pony as if it were a present for the pair of us. It was she who provided him with a name, Black Prince, and when Andy taught us to ride him she learned faster. She was older, of course.

The Master's own horse was a big gray gelding named Sea King. Andy called him willful, but he seemed docile with the Master's hands on the reins. I had only looked on from a respectful distance and found it hard to take in Andy's instruction that I was to join him.

"Join him, how? Walk alongside?"

"On Black Prince, fool." Andy pushed up the forelock which disguised a bald patch on the top of his head. "And mind you don't discredit me by riding like a sack of seaweed." He grinned unpleasantly. "Else I might send the Demons after you again."

The direction was for meeting at North Point. As I came up to him, I said, "Good day, Master," and put a hand to my forelock. He nodded silently and clicked his tongue for Sea King to walk on.

For several hundred yards the path lay inland, before emerging to where the sea lay directly beneath us. He halted there. The western cloud had thickened, but the day was mild still.

The Master spoke abruptly. "That was a fine caterwauling you treated us to last night."

I was thrown once more into confusion. The Master's quarters were at the far end of the house, and it had not occurred to me he too might have been wakened.

"I'm sorry, sir . . ."

He stared down at me. He was more than six feet tall, his horse better than seventeen hands to

Black Prince's thirteen and a half. Letting go the reins, he rubbed his hands together slowly.

"You have put on some height in the past year. How much?"

I had no trouble answering that. At the foot of the back stairs, pencil lines on the plaster marked where Paddy and I measured one another, regularly on birthdays and quite often in between.

"Three inches, sir. Well, above two."

He nodded. "Are you happy here?"

His voice was deep, and his manner of speaking strange. As Mother Ryan's was, but in her case we knew the reason—she was proud of being born and raised in Ireland. The Master's accent did not resemble either hers or the local one, which was also my own. It took me a moment to grasp the question, and "here" perplexed me. Where else should I be?

I said quickly, "Yes indeed, sir."

"It's a small place for a growing boy. You have wanted education."

Again I was puzzled. This was the spring holiday, but normally Paddy and I were taken daily to school on Sheriff's in Joe's fishing dinghy.

I said, "I was second to top in my reading class. And Roger Burton who came top is six months older."

He smiled, but it was bleak. "And what do you read, in that class you speak of?"

"All sorts of things. *Duties and Obediences, The Torments of Hell, The Infidels of the North . . .*"

"Would you say you learn matters of value from these books?"

An honest answer would have been very little if anything, but I knew better than to be strictly honest to a questioning adult, particularly to the Master.

"Yes, sir."

"I am told you dreamed of Demons last night. Do the books tell you of them?"

I nodded. "Yes, they do."

"What do they say?"

He sounded as though he really wanted to know, which in itself surprised me. I had taken it for granted that, with a large room lined ceiling to floor with books, he must be the wisest person I knew—far wiser than our teachers, or Mr. Hawkins the Summoner, or Sheriff Wilson. But he had put the question, and I had better answer it.

"They tell us Demons are the minions of the Dark One. They come to warn men against transgression of the laws, and to punish those who persist in wickedness."

He looked at me until I felt uncomfortable. At last, he said, "I have served you ill."

That puzzled me even more. How could the Master serve me, or want to? I kept silent, and he went on, "It may not be too late. We will talk again, perhaps of Demons. Now it is time for your tea."

I followed him back on Black Prince, disturbed but intrigued. Would the talk be in his library? I had ventured there once while he was away on Sheriff's, and the close-packed volumes had fascinated me. There was even a set of wooden steps, spiraling around a pole, to get at those too high to reach. Mother Ryan had caught me peering and pulled me away by the ear. It was, she scolded with a sharp tweak, a spot forbidden to any but the Master.

. . .

All this took place on Tuesday. The new term started on Friday, which meant just one day before the weekend break. I had fingers crossed for our camping trip: The weather had broken, and Mother Ryan fastened our oilskins on a rain-smeared morning. Joe greeted us at the jetty.

"You're late. That's a bad beginning to the term."

"No more than five minutes," Paddy said. "Liza had her kittens in the night. Joe, she's got *five,* and we saw the last one born! Two black-and-white, two tortoiseshell, and one a funny gray color. We're calling it Smoky."

That had been my suggestion. It was usually Paddy who thought of names, always Paddy who decided what the name was going to be.

Joe said, "Never mind cats and kittens. Cast off, Ben. I've done a day's work before you were stirring, and another's waiting."

The dinghy smelled of the catch he had landed earlier, a tang of fish mixed with salt and sweat and tobacco. Joe was almost as tall as the Master, and broader, with a battered face and a big nose and thick black beard. He set sail to catch the stiff northwesterly, and we heaved our way across the bay with gusts of rain stinging our faces. I glanced surreptitiously at Paddy. I had got over being seasick, but she still suffered occasionally. She seemed all right this morning.

I looked back toward the house, where smoke rose from two small chimneys at the north end and a larger one at the south. The Master would be sitting by his study fire, drinking the coffee Mother Ryan took him about this time. I'd never tasted coffee—it was not for the likes of us, Mother Ryan said—but loved the smell. Perhaps he would be reading one of his thousands of books. I wondered when the summons for the talk might come.

This being the first day of school, Sheriff Wilson addressed us. He reminded us of our duty: to obey our parents and those in authority, all adults, in word and deed and thought. We were to work hard and to learn—learn especially those things through which we might escape the wrath of the Dark One, in this life and the life to come. Work hard, and learn well!

He too was big, but fleshy. He had a high

forehead, fat cheeks, and spectacles whose lenses had no rims. He picked me out as I headed toward the classroom.

"Young Ben of Old Isle! How are you, boy?"

"Well, sir. Thank you, sir."

He was smiling, but he smiled easily. People said he was the best Sheriff in living memory, more easygoing than his predecessors. The stocks which stood across the green from his house were empty more often than not. I thought I ought to like him, but could not.

"The Master is well, I hope?"

The tone was solicitous, but I didn't believe the hope was honest. I had once observed him in conversation with the Master, and though I could not distinguish their words, there had been contempt in the Master's voice, wheedling unease in the Sheriff's.

I said, "He is well, sir."

"Respect him, boy. He is a great man."

"Indeed he is!"

I spoke warmly and thought his eyes narrowed behind the rimless lenses, but he smiled still more widely and patted my head to send me on my way.

. . .

Although I would not have preferred to live there, I found Sheriff's an exciting place. Apart from ruinous mounds from the days of the Madness, fascinating forbidden territory, there was the bustle of people, and there were shops. The *Hesperus*, which took produce to the mainland and brought back other goods, had recently returned. Paddy and I found mainland sweets tastier than the Widow Barnes's fudge, and with hoarded pennies we bought sticks of toffee studded with hazelnuts. We munched our way happily to the quay, where Joe was waiting for us.

I began to rattle off an account of the day, but Paddy interrupted.

"What is it, Joe? What's wrong?"

When I looked, his expression was troubled. He turned his head away.

"Nothing that won't wait. We've a tide to catch."

She grasped his arm. "Tell us now."

I envied her manner of commanding him. He stared unhappily. "Well, you'll have to know. It's the Master."

"What about him?" I asked.

But Paddy had read Joe's face. "Not *dead?*"

"No," I said. "That can't be!"

Yet now I could read his grimness too, and knew it was.